KT-549-587

To renew, find us online at:
https://capitadiscovery.co.uk/bromley

Please note: Items from the adult library
may also accrue overdue charges when
borrowed on children's tickets.

In partnership with

the feel good place

Scholastic Children's Books
An imprint of Scholastic Ltd
Euston House, 24 Eversholt Street, London, NW1 1DB, UK
Registered office: Westfield Road, Southam, Warwickshire, CV47 0RA
SCHOLASTIC and associated logos are trademarks and/or
registered trademarks of Scholastic Inc.

First published in the UK by Scholastic Ltd, 2020

ISBN 978 1407 19571 1

A CIP catalogue record for this book
is available from the British Library.

Printed and bound by CPI Group (UK) Ltd, Croydon, CR0 4YY
Papers used by Scholastic Children's Books are made
from wood grown in sustainable forests.

1 3 5 7 9 10 8 6 4 2

www.scholastic.co.uk

THE
ACCIDENTAL
WIZARD

KIMBERLY PAULEY

ILLUSTRATED BY JASON COCKCROFT

SCHOLASTIC

For my mother, Helen (1945 – 2020), for always taking me to the library when I was little, and for the librarians who let me check out more books than I was allowed.

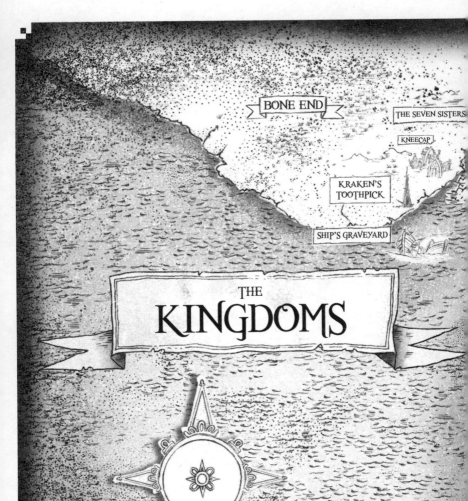

BONE END

THE SEVEN SISTERS

KNEECAP

KRAKEN'S TOOTHPICK

SHIP'S GRAVEYARD

THE KINGDOMS

THE EYE OF THE SEA

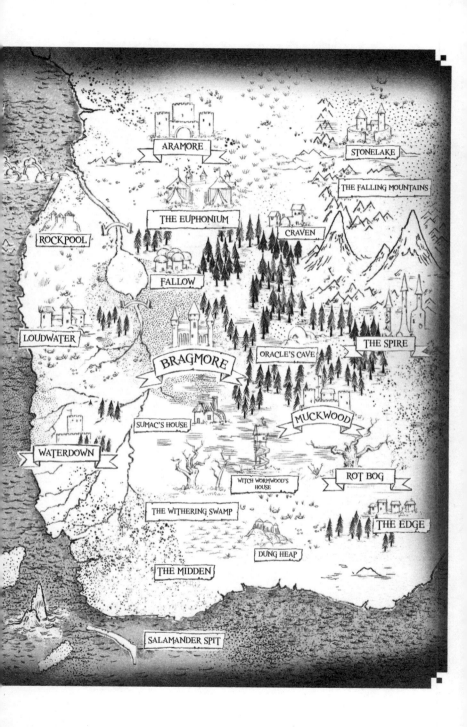

1

IN WHICH A SMALL ACCIDENT BECOMES A BIG PROBLEM

There was a shattering of glass.

"Duck!" shouted Ripplemintz the Sage.

Twig looked around in confusion. "Where?"

They were in the tallest tower of the castle, where the wizard both lived and conducted his often unintentionally hazardous magical experiments. It was certainly *no* place for a duck. The only place for a duck in the whole castle was surely the kitchens, which would be a very unfortunate location to find oneself in if you were, in fact, a duck.

"No, I meant *get down*!" yelled Ripplemintz.

Twig didn't need any further warning. He dropped the book he'd been reading and flattened himself against the floor just in time to avoid something very fast and vaguely sparkly that whooshed over his head, messed up his hair, and continued out the window. There was no glass to break *there*, at least, it having been blown out last winter during a particularly unruly experiment.

"What *was* that?" Twig asked as he stood up and dusted himself off.

Ripplemintz climbed down off a sturdy wooden table (the sparse furnishings in the tower had to be strong or they didn't survive) and gave his robes a quick check. He seemed a bit sheepish, but that might have just been the way his curly beard made him look.

"*Errrhhhrrm,*" he said. "That was just a little boast, a bit of hyperbole, if you will. A small accidental spell I've been storing that got away from me," he added, noting Twig's expression.

"A boast? You mean, like showing off?" asked Twig. Sometimes he wasn't sure if his mentor was teasing him or just being strange.

"*Yes,*" said Ripplemintz, rather testily. "One of mine,

if you must know. I was young once, after all, just like you. I'd forgotten it was even up there – it's been bottled up all this time . . ." He flicked a bit of imaginary dust off his long purple robes and looked thoughtful. "I *do* hope it hasn't grown."

Twig nodded, not at what the sage *had* said, but at what he *hadn't*. For instance, Ripplemintz *hadn't* said:

1. That words have power and so you need to keep a close eye on them. If you don't watch what you say, especially if you are a wizard, things have a tendency to happen. *Explosive* things in particular.

2. What *type* of accidental spell it had been. Had he once, in a youthful daze, claimed the sky to be bluer than it was? Had he said the king was taller or the queen was prettier or that the kingdom of Muckwood was the best in all the land (which it certainly wasn't)? The *type* of spell made all the difference, after all.

Exactly how long had it been trapped in that bottle, anyway? Words had a habit of getting away from Ripplemintz, even now that he was the official Court Wizard in Residence. This was probably why he was stuck in the tiny, remote kingdom of Muckwood to begin with. Everyone knew that the most powerful wizards in the world – like the celebrated Kudzu of the Spire, and brave Pumice Pummelstone of Aramore – lived in large coastal kingdoms or near the gem-rich Falling Mountains.

Twig reflected that Ripplemintz also hadn't said what they were going to *do* about the escaped spell, although he already knew the answer to that question. He, as the wizard's sole remaining (surviving) apprentice, would have to clean up the mess.

4

Ripplemintz had already turned back to whatever it was he'd been working on before the spell had taken flight.

"Off you go then, Twig," he said, waving the boy away. "Be sure to take the number three net and one of the large containment bottles . . . perhaps a green or blue. Definitely not a clear one, I'm running low on those."

Twig gathered up some supplies and stopped only long enough to look out of the window the accidental spell had exited by. It overlooked the gardens and stables, and he could see that an apple tree had caught fire along one edge of the gardens.

A few stable boys were trying to put it out rather ineffectually by throwing hay at it. That looked like as good a place to start as any.

"*Do* hurry," said Ripplemintz. "We don't want it running into anything important."

Twig headed through the door and down the long, *long* flight of steps that led out of the tower. By the time he reached the gardens, yet another apple tree had caught on fire and everything smelled a bit like burnt apple pie.

"Did you perhaps see something sparkly go shooting by here?" Twig asked one of the stable boys. "Probably right before the tree caught fire?"

"Oh, aye," said the boy, who looked like he was rather enjoying the spectacle. "I was walking Old Thomas in the courtyard – he likes apples, y'see – and I led him over to get one, when this *thing* comes *whizzing* by us. Hit Old Tom right on the head, it did, and then bounced off into the tree and set it on fire!"

Old Thomas was the king's favourite warhorse, though he was so old now that he was only trotted out on fancy occasions, such as when a neighbouring king came to visit. It had been a very long time since that had happened.

"Is Old Thomas all right?" asked Twig with a sinking feeling. If anything had happened to the horse, the king would not be pleased and Ripplemintz would surely blame it on him somehow. King Mervyn was seldom pleased with either of them. He thought magic was a complete waste of time, and would have done away with the position of court wizard completely if it hadn't been for all the other kingdoms being so proud of theirs. Twig wasn't all that fond of working for Ripplemintz, but it *was* better than living off acorns in the forest.

"See for yourself," said the boy, pulling Twig out of his thoughts and pointing into the paddock. Twig stared in disbelief.

Old Thomas was nearly unrecognizable! He was cantering around in circles, his head held high and his mane and tail flowing in a particularly magnificent way. Three stable boys were trying to catch him, with very little success. He neighed in blatant triumph and then leapt over a fence and galloped off towards the forest.

"Oh," said Twig. "I guess he's OK then."

"Stable Master says he ain't never seen anything like it. Old Thomas is nearly thirty years old, y'know. He ain't moved like that since ... well, since before either one of us was born."

Twig squared his shoulders. What *exactly* had

Ripplemintz let loose?

"Well. Did you happen to see which way the, er, thing went?"

The boy pointed towards the middle of the garden where the statuary maze was located. Then he wandered off and half-heartedly chucked some more hay on the burning trees.

Twig skirted carefully around the fire, where servants from the kitchen were now running about with buckets of water and slopping most of it on the ground, and entered the gardens from the South Gate, since that was the one furthest away from the kelpie pond, and he didn't feel like being drowned today.

He hadn't gone far when he ran into what seemed to be the next victim of Ripplemintz's escaped spell – though victim was, perhaps, not *quite* the right word, because standing on what used to be a statue of the king was the largest gnome Twig had *ever* seen. All that was left of the homage to King Mervyn was the stone base. The statue itself had been shattered, and chunks of marble lay scattered in the grass. The gnome was the size of a largish toddler, which put him at about five or six times the size of a normal garden-variety gnome. Rather than attempting to hide when Twig came upon him, he stood even taller and actually flexed his muscles.

"Ye there!" bellowed the gnome, which was very non-gnome-like indeed.

"Me?" asked Twig.

"Yes, ye! I am Glimfinkle Cogfuzz Clickkettle the Fourteenth, King of the Garden Gnomes! Bring me something to eat!"

"Er . . ." said Twig.

"You ain't the king," piped up a small voice from behind a rosebush. "Dinkwizz Swiftsteel is!"

A normal-sized gnome poked his head out. He was small enough to completely disappear behind a large rose.

"Not any more!" roared Glimfinkle. His round,

chubby cheeks were bright red, matching his hat. His shouting reminded Twig of when his little brother Tadpole would throw a tantrum, except that Tadpole didn't have a long white beard.

"You can't just go and declare yourself king," said another tiny voice, and a petite (even for a gnome) woman emerged from behind a rock.

"Oh yes I can, Sprinkl Fittzspark! Just look at me!" shouted Glimfinkle, with his hands on his pudgy hips. "I am the best gnome there ever was! How can I *not* be king?!" He turned to Twig and pointed at him. "Bring me a feast! I wants a feast! With pudding! *Lots* of pudding! The kind with sprinkles on!"

As Glimfinkle shouted, more and more gnomes were sticking their little heads out of unlikely hiding places. Twig had never realized before exactly how many gnomes lived in the gardens. Now he understood why Ripplemintz had often said the place was infested. They normally kept to themselves, but right now they all looked really annoyed. At least their annoyance was directed at Glimfinkle, who was parading like a peacock around the base of the statue.

Twig got down on his knees so he could talk to the little gnome woman who was staring angrily up at Glimfinkle and shaking her fist. "What happened to him?" he asked her, though he suspected that he knew the answer.

Sprinkl clucked her tongue. "Glimfinkle was sunning himself up on that statue, like he always does, the lazy sot. And then there was a flash of light and BOOM!" She clapped her small hands together. "The statue's gone to bits and Glimfinkle got blowed up!"

"Blowed up?"

She wagged her tiny finger at Twig. "That's what I said! Just look at him! He's not even proper gnome-size any more. He's bigger than a bloomin' brownie, for heaven's sake! And looks like his head's gone big as well. Thinking he's the boggin' king now." Sprinkl shook her head, looking as disgusted as someone that small could look.

Scores of gnomes had surrounded Glimfinkle so that they could argue with him, and a few had climbed up on to the base of the statue. A number of them had even taken out their swords, which were the size of toothpicks but had quite a wicked point. It looked like there was about to be a small-scale war.

Twig stood up, stepped carefully over the gathering gnomes, and picked up Glimfinkle, holding him under his arms and keeping him at arm's length. The gnome kicked like a baby and tried to pummel Twig with his fists but couldn't quite reach.

"I think perhaps you need a time out," said Twig. He looked around, unsure of what to do with the oversized gnome that he had in his hands. He didn't have time to take him back to Ripplemintz for sorting out, not when he had to track down the escaped spell before things got even worse than a gnome with grand aspirations, so he simply walked over to a nearby tree and hung the kicking gnome from a branch by his braces. "I'll be back later to shrink you down to normal size," he said to Glimfinkle.

"No!" said Glimfinkle, amid loud cheers from the other gnomes. A few of them were even pegging him with small pebbles.

"Yes," replied Twig. "And you lot, don't go, er, killing him or anything." The cheering died down a bit then, which was worrisome.

"Which way did the flashy light thing go?" he asked Sprinkl.

"Oh, it flew off into the maze," she said. "You can hear it bangin' around in there, can't you?"

Now that she mentioned it, Twig *could* hear something. It sounded large and fizzly and very, *very* fast. He sighed, squared his shoulders and entered the maze. The longer magic ran amuck, the worse it got. He needed to catch that accidental spell as soon as he could.

2

IN WHICH SOMETHING DOESN'T BLOW UP

The Muckwood Maze was not world-famous like the Glammerock Maze (which had been magically grown from rare crystals and gems) and it wasn't nearly as large as the one at Cornerstone Castle in Aramore (which was so big that visitors got lost in it on a regular basis). It didn't have rare and exotic plants growing in it like the one at the Spire that had been built by a long-forgotten fairy tribe. But the hedges were lush and tall, and it was home to a multitude of the creatures that called Muckwood home – such as boggle-boos, derricks, pixies and leprechauns, not to mention squirrels. They were all quite titchy, not overly clever, prone to territorial disputes and, except for the pixies that delivered messages via Pixie Post, not very friendly to people.

Twig turned right, left and then right again in the maze. That was where he found a squirrel, busy preening a long, ridiculously luxurious tail that looked like it belonged on something much grander than a squirrel. He turned left and saw a leprechaun chortling gleefully to himself as he pulled an over-full pot of gold behind him. A few more turns found Twig barely avoiding a growing swarm of boggle-boos battling with a contingent of well-armed pixies, all of them shouting incomprehensible insults at each other that had something to do with conquering the world.

Twig had just edged around a corner to escape the battle when he heard a whizzing crash ahead of him. Running forwards, he finally saw what had become of the loose spell. Unfortunately, it could no longer be accurately described as little because it was now a *huge* rolling ball of fizzing magical energy, spitting out sparks and coming straight for him. Twig sighed. There was no *way* it was going to fit into the containment bottle he'd brought along. It wouldn't have fit into *ten* containment bottles.

Twig held up his net and began chanting the containment spell anyway, for lack of anything better to do. He threw in a hopeful anti-explosion twist too, just in case. Ripplemintz was always yelling at him about improvising, but it wasn't the old sage who was standing in the maze between a really, *really* large accidental spell gone wild and a horde of battling faerie folk.

The spell rolled faster and faster towards him, picking up speed. Was it getting even *bigger* as it neared him? The edges of it were almost like flames, brushing against the hedges on either side. It crackled. It sputtered. It extended octopus-like tendrils towards him, almost like it was reaching right for him. He'd never seen anything like it.

Twig gulped, braced himself and hoped, at the very least, that the anti-explosion bit of his spell would work. He squeezed his eyes shut at the last minute and held the uselessly small net steady in front of him. The ball of energy bowled right into him with a loud WHOMP that could surely be heard from one end of Muckwood to the other.

There was a brief silence before pixie war cries filled the air as they resumed battle. They were a single-minded race, as were the boggle-boos (there were debates over whether boggle-boos actually had a brain), and nothing short of being knocked unconscious would keep them from fighting once they had started.

Twig carefully opened his eyes. He blinked. All that remained of the net was a small pile of ash. The containment bottle had disintegrated. The spell seemed to have disappeared as well. He patted himself down to make sure all his body parts were still attached and un-singed.

Where had Ripplemintz's spell gone? He scratched his head. Had it rolled right through him and back into the pixie's battlefield? He crept to the corner and peered around it, but the battle was exactly as he had last seen it: a furious mass of winged pixies embroiled in heated battle with an equal number of enraged

bubble-eyed boggle-boos, with more still arriving.

Had the spell bounced off of him and gone back the other way? No, he'd definitely felt it go *through* him. It wasn't a feeling one could forget: warm and tingly, like bathing in hot chocolate. He put a hand to his chest, imagining he could still feel it. He looked up into the cloudless blue sky. Other than a few pixies darting about, it was clear. It hadn't flown up. Where had it gone?

Twig suddenly found himself very annoyed. Why was *he* always the one who had to clean up Ripplemintz's messes? Yes, he was the old sage's apprentice, but surely no apprentice had *ever* had to put up with as much as he had to. He even had to trim the sage's gnarly toenails! He bet Pumice of Aramore didn't make *his* apprentices (and, yes, he had more than one!) do that. *No one* should have to do that. *And* Ripplemintz barely ever bothered teaching him magic. Pretty much all Twig knew he had taught himself from the sage's books, and by being quiet and paying attention.

"*Enough!*" shouted Twig. "I have absolutely *had it!*" He even stamped his foot. Ripplemintz wasn't there to hear it, but it still made him feel better. Maybe his little brother Tadpole was on to something. He gave another stomp for good measure.

It took Twig a moment to realize the noise of the pitched battle had suddenly died away. Stepping all the way around the corner to get a better look, he saw that the pixies and boggle-boos had all mysteriously stopped. A nearby pixie rolled its eyes up to try and

get a look at him, but otherwise every single one of the little fairy folk was completely frozen in place. A boggle-boo near him was stuck mid-punch, a pixie's fist embedded in his tiny face. Another was caught flipped upside down in the air, her greenish-blue hair going in every direction like she'd been hit by lightning.

"You," said Twig, pointing at the pixie who'd tried to look at him. "Tell me who did this to you?"

The pixie appeared to be suddenly released from whatever was holding her in place. She shook herself cautiously and gave Twig a respectful curtsy. "I think you did, sir, wizard, sir," she said.

"Me?" said Twig.

"Begging your pardon, sir. I've the Sight and I can tell by looking at you that you're the world's greatest wizard. If not you, then who?"

"Me?" said Twig again. Everything else aside, no one had ever called him "sir" before.

He wondered for a second if he was dreaming or had, in fact, been knocked out by the

spell as it had rolled over him. Or maybe he'd died and gone to heaven – except he'd always understood the afterlife to involve things like fluffy clouds and harp music, and there was none of that.

The pixie nervously jittered from foot to foot. "We're very sorry about the mess, sir, and do apologise. If you'll just let us all free, we'll get to work cleaning up right away."

"*I'm* not stopping you," said Twig, waving his hand. But as soon as he said the words and waved, the pixies and boggle-boos became unfrozen. The ones that had been trapped mid-leap fell flat to the ground with a squeak.

"Thank you, sir, wizard, sir!" said the pixie, curtseying repeatedly in the air as she flew backwards at full speed. Before Twig could reply, they had all picked up their fallen comrades and disappeared to wherever they had come from. If there was one thing every kind of fairy was good at, it was disappearing, especially if they thought trouble was brewing or they might get roped into doing something they didn't want to do.

Twig stood in the now abandoned space and looked around. It was dead quiet. Eerily quiet. He was pretty sure he could feel the eyes of hundreds of fairy folk upon him. He stared at the hand he'd waved with. The last time he'd had a run in with a pixie, it had tried to steal his socks. It definitely hadn't called him sir.

He snapped his fingers. A spark of magical energy flew off and disappeared in a flash. Something was definitely going on, but he didn't *feel* any different. Except, he *did* feel quite . . . confident. Feeling taller, he strode off through the maze and back to the tree where he'd hung up Glimfinkle.

The larger-than-he-should-be gnome was still where he had left him, though he was a bit worse for wear, as the other gnomes had apparently pelted him with leftover bits of semi-rotten food before leaving him hanging there by himself. Twig pointed a finger at the gnome, made a swooping motion with his hand, and said, *"Back to normal with you!"* in what he hoped was a suitably wizard-y sounding voice.

He hadn't totally expected anything to happen, but something did. Glimfinkle was lifted off the tree, swirled around in the air a few times, and then brought gently to his feet. By the time he touched the ground, he was back to his normal size. He took one look at Twig and hightailed it into a dense rose bush with a muttered curse or two. Twig heard a stampede of tiny footsteps as the gnomes hiding in the brush fled.

Twig made it back to the tower without further incident, stopping only to put out the last remaining bit of fire with a few waves of his hands and a well-placed word or two, much to the amazement of the stable boys. He trudged halfway up the stairs, paused in thought a minute, muttered, *"Flit, flight, float,"* and then floated the rest of the way up.

Twig opened the door with just a twitch of his finger and paused to consider. Ripplemintz had barely moved since he'd left. The sage was twiddling with a crucible full of something bubbling and molten, just like normal. But things weren't normal. *He* wasn't normal.

"Ripplemintz?"

"Hmmm?" said the sage, not looking up. "Did you sort everything out then, Twig?"

"Um, yes, pretty much," said Twig, which was

technically true. He hadn't put Old Thomas back to normal, but somehow he thought the king might like his newly restored horse better anyway. "Except, I was wondering . . . if someone were to use a containment spell but the bottle broke and you didn't have anything else to direct it to, what do you think might happen?"

Ripplemintz dripped a few drops of some revolting-looking greenish-purple liquid into the crucible and it started to smoke.

"That is a very interesting question," he said. "If someone were foolish enough to do that, I suppose they might find that *they themselves* became the container."

"Ah," said Twig. He suspected that he now knew where the no-longer-little accidental spell had wound up. "I was also wondering . . . Do you remember what exactly that bit of boastful hyperbole whatnot you accidentally cast was?"

Ripplemintz straightened up, one hand to his back, and stretched. There was a bit of a pop as his old bones readjusted themselves. He chuckled to himself.

"Oh, yes, I remember it very well. I wasn't much older than you and, like most young wizards, I thought a lot of myself back then. Thought I was the greatest wizard there ever was and wasn't afraid to say it." Then he got a good look at Twig, his eyes going wide as he saw his apprentice floating above the floor. "Oh, my," he said. "I suppose it's safe to say that my little accidental spell grew quite big, eh?"

Twig nodded. It was weird, being the world's greatest wizard. But, so far, he rather liked it.

3

IN WHICH TWIG LOOKS A GIFT HORSE IN THE MOUTH

The first day of being the world's greatest wizard was very, very exciting for Twig. Ripplemintz tested Twig every which way he knew how. He started him off with small spells – vanishing all the dust in the tower, mending the broken furniture and automagically alphabetizing the sage's extensive collection of spell books. Twig suspected an ulterior motive, but was happy enough to not have to do any of the work non-magically that he didn't complain. Then they moved on to levitating things around the tower one by one until Twig had every piece of furniture dancing at once.

Twig blew things up and then put them back together. He conjured firework dragons and illusory trolls (seriously startling a passing chambermaid). He made their simple bread and cheese lunch into a feast fit for a king. He even created music out of thin air until half the castle were tapping their toes.

The entire castle wondered at the shows of sparks and the conjured creatures that flew out of the windows of the old tower. Muckwood had never seen so much (successful) magic in its entire history – and certainly not since Ripplemintz had been hired.

The second day was quite a bit busier, as the residents of the castle began inventing reasons to climb up all the stairs to the tower to find out what, exactly, was going on. First it was a curious page, then one of the scullery girls, then a few stable boys. After that, the news spread everywhere and a stream of out-of-breath visitors kept arriving, all of them wanting to see the spectacle up close.

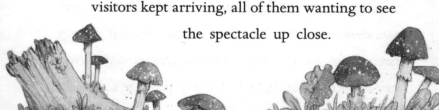

Of course, Twig was happy to oblige. No one had ever paid him much attention – before he had been taken on as Ripplemintz's apprentice, he'd simply been the sixth child in a string of twelve born to ne'er-do-well Nettle and Hedge Thicket. Afterwards, he'd been known around the castle as "that apprentice wot hadn't been blowed up yet".

But it was Old Thomas that really made people look at him differently. One of the visiting stable boys had recognized Twig as the one who'd come around when the horse had undergone his miraculous transformation. Old Thomas was still running free. No one had been able to catch him. Then the leprechaun with his overfull pot of wealth had stumbled out of the maze, drunk on gold. And there were rumours of a gnome grumbling about the upstart wizard boy who'd made him big and then small again.

Suddenly, people weren't just visiting. They were asking. Asking for things to be mended, things to be improved, things to be scryed. Mostly small things, which was good, as magic had its limits; you couldn't make something out of nothing, though you could completely change what you had to make it better or combine different things into something amazing.

Some time late in the day, Ripplemintz barred the door shut right in the face of a startled chambermaid who'd come up to ask for a fancy new dress.

"What did you do *that* for?" asked Twig. He was a bit tired from working all of the magic, but mostly he felt good. The best he'd ever felt, in fact.

"Don't you realize what you've done, Twig?" said Ripplemintz, twirling the end of his beard around his finger like he did when he was trying to figure out why some bit of magic wasn't doing what he expected it to do.

"I've made people happy," said Twig. "What's the harm in that?"

"You'll learn soon enough that it is both inadvisable and impossible to make everyone happy all the time or even, by Milkweed's beard, some of the time. But that's beside the point. What do you think will happen when the people you've helped today – for *free*, mind – tell all of their friends and word gets around that you're handing out magical favours?"

"Well ..." began Twig and then stopped. He had suddenly pictured his parents and all his eleven brothers and sisters appearing on his doorstep. Tadpole would want toys. The twins would ask for sweets. His mum would want, well, everything and then a bit more, if it were for free. And his oldest brother, Badger, was always trying some new get-rich-quick scheme, no matter how often they turned around and bit him on the bum, like that time he'd tried to farm squirrels.

"Oh, yes," said Ripplemintz, sagely nodding his head. "I see you understand now."

Twig shuffled his feet. "It was only a few people around the castle, not the village. Maybe it won't be that bad."

Turns out, it was worse.

Word spread beyond the castle faster than Twig would have thought possible. By lunchtime, most of his family, including cousins so far removed he wasn't even sure he was related to them at all, had come to visit, demanding magical favours.

Ripplemintz put a sign on the door and barred it, but not even that stopped them hammering away.

"Maybe if I . . .?" began Twig.

"*Absolutely not,*" said Ripplemintz. "Don't you see how bad it is already? We're going to have to work out a schedule and payment terms and all kinds of things, none of this willy-nilly business or it'll always be like this. They'll *never* leave you alone."

"I know you're in there, Twig!" came a voice from the other side of the door. It was his mum. He could tell by the way the back of his neck tingled.

"It's my mum. Maybe just . . ."

"NO," said Ripplemintz, but then he softened his voice. "Family is the worst. Trust me, I know. You'll never have a moment's peace if you don't set some boundaries."

"I heard that!" came the voice.

"Good!" said Ripplemintz, but Twig noticed he double-checked the bar on the door.

"Sorry," whispered Twig. "Her ears are really good. She can hear if you miss the chamber pot, no matter where she is." His older brother Stick had tested this extensively. Twig hadn't missed *him* at all when he'd moved out.

"Yes, well," said Ripplemintz. He cleared his throat and backed away from the door a bit. Twig's mum had that effect on a lot of people.

Nettle Thicket was a sharp woman, in the same manner as a spade or scythe. Where Twig's father Hedge was a bit of a dreamer, his mum was very practical. And stout. Like a barrel, with a voice to match.

"I DID NOT come up all these bloomin' steps to be turned away at the DOOR!" she shouted from outside.

She knocked on the door again. It shook.

Twig looked at Ripplemintz. The sage stared back at him, blinking slowly. He took another step away from the door.

"Well, maybe just this once. She *is* your mum, after all," said Ripplemintz. "But no more after this one!"

Twig opened the door with a sigh and let his mother in. She was followed by the rest of his immediate family, all eleven brothers and sisters, the wives of his two older brothers, their three children, and, lastly, his father Hedge, struggling to carry a fat pig that had a bandage on its foot.

"Bacon's gone a bit lame," his dad said apologetically, "and you know how much your mum loves him."

Twig did know. He fixed Bacon first.

Three hours, four picnic hampers full of food, and a lot of new clothes later, the Thickets finally left, but Twig knew they'd be back like a bad penny.

Exhausted, Twig went to bed early, but had only just fallen asleep when a magpie flew through a window and landed on top of his head as he lay sleeping on his pallet in a corner of the tower. It wasn't the best way to wake up, though it did beat sharing a bed with his brother Tadpole, who still wasn't quite toilet trained. That was one of the reasons he'd taken the apprenticeship to begin with – pretty much anything beat waking up in a wet bed with a toddler's feet kicking you in the face.

"Aaaaagh!" Twig screamed as the magpie squawked and tried to untangle its feet from his hair.

"Woah! Watch where yer flappin'!" said a little

voice that sounded vaguely familiar. "I've only got the one me!"

The magpie hopped free and landed on Twig's stomach, which was when he saw that a gnome was on the back of the bird, riding in a tiny, hand-stitched mouse leather saddle.

"Glimfinkle? What do *you* want?" asked Twig, more than a bit surprised.

The gnome leapt out of the saddle and stomped his way up Twig's chest in his little fur-lined red boots. The bird flew off like he knew what was coming and wanted none of it.

"What do I want? *What do I want?* I want what yer took from me!"

He shook a finger at Twig's nose. "I was big, I was! I was grand! Now I'm just . . . look at me!"

He grabbed Twig's nose, so close now that Twig had to squint and close   one

eye to even see him at all. "I'm tiny again!"

Twig sat up, and Glimfinkle tumbled ingloriously down into his lap. "Well, you're a *gnome*. Gnomes are tiny. That's who you are."

The gnome scrambled to his feet. "Says who?"

Twig stared down at him. "Everyone?"

"*Pfffft*. Who cares about everyone? What do they know?"

Twig didn't know what to say to that. He'd often wondered something similar himself.

The gnome stepped back and closed his eyes like he was bracing himself for something. "I've come so ye can make me big again."

Twig stared at him.

"Twig? Are you all right? What was all that ruckus? Why is there a bird flying around the room?" Ripplemintz stepped out from behind the wooden screen that separated Twig's bed from the rest of the tower.

"It's, er, Glimfinkle's bird. He came in through the window on it."

"And what, exactly, is a Glimfinkle?" asked the sage, fumbling to find his glasses.

"A gnome," said Twig.

"The King of the Gnomes!" said Glimfinkle, thrusting out his chest.

"No, you're not," said Twig. "You know you're not."

"But I *should* be," Glimfinkle glowered. "If you hadn't gone and mucked with things, I would be."

Twig sincerely doubted that, but he held his tongue.

Ripplemintz had found his glasses finally, hidden in one of his long sleeves, where he kept important things and snacks.

"Ah, I see," he said. "You must be the gnome that Twig here told me about. The one that had been struck by . . . ah, the . . . er . . . mysterious magical force that escaped the tower the other day."

They had both agreed that it was perhaps best to *not* mention exactly what it was that had gone barrelling through Muckwood. Twig suspected Ripplemintz was worried about what the king would say.

"Aye," said the gnome. "And I've come because I want what I had back." He stared at Twig. "Word's getting around. I know ye can do it. Yer the most powerful wizard ever been seen around these parts.

Maybe anywhere."

Twig looked at Ripplemintz and raised an eyebrow. What harm would it do, just one gnome? But the old sage shook his head. "No more willy-nilly magic without thinking about the consequences, Twig," he said. "We talked about this already."

"Sorry," said Twig to Glimfinkle, shrugging his shoulders.

The persistent gnome argued with them until Ripplemintz threatened to have Twig make him smaller instead of bigger. That sent him packing.

After Ripplemintz had barred the door *and* windows, Twig collapsed on to a chair. "What am I going to *do?*" he asked the sage. "This is the worst thing ever. It's like a curse – like when those fairies show up at christenings and give out ridiculous gifts that sound good until you actually use them!"

"Oh, now," said Ripplemintz, "there are plenty of wizards out there who would kill their own nan to have the kind of power that you've got." He patted Twig on the shoulder.

"As a matter of fact, rumour is Sumac Crabapple did just that, though he might regret it now. His granny was a very accomplished hag and he was cursed with festering boils." Ripplemintz stared thoughtfully up at the ceiling. "So, just remember, it could be worse. I saw him at the last Euphonium and he had a particularly rancid-looking carbuncle right on the tip of his nose. It was practically purple."

There was a sharp rap on the door.

"I'm tired! Go away!" yelled Twig. He was nearly positive it was Badger. His brother had been trying to show him a "brand new" kind of squirrel trap that looked exactly like the old kind of trap.

There was a loud "Hummpppphfff" from the other side of the door and then a sheet of parchment was slid underneath. Ripplemintz picked it up.

"Hm," he said. "You know, I shouldn't have said that, about how things could be worse." He handed the paper to Twig. "It seems you have been requested by the king."

4

IN WHICH TWIG MEETS THE KING EVEN THOUGH HE DOESN'T WANT TO

Twig had been living in the castle for around a year, but he'd never been anywhere near the throne room. He knew the back-ways and the servant's quarters and, of course, the kitchens, but the great hall and the throne room had been off limits to anyone without an impressive title. He'd only ever seen the ruler of Muckwood once from afar, when the nobles had gone on their annual wild boar hunt in the Eternal Forest. King Mervyn had looked quite imposing astride his horse, his red velvet fur-lined cape draped around him.

You'd never know from looking at him that Muckwood was the least impressive of all the kingdoms.

The throne room was smaller than the great hall, but still a much larger and grander room than Twig had ever seen before. He was glad Ripplemintz had made him magic up some new clothing and boots, even though they itched as he'd had only some old burlap, a tablecloth and corn husks to work with. He didn't have much time to look around as the herald herded him through the room, but he had a general impression of lots of tapestries and cushions and well-dressed lords and ladies twittering to themselves behind their hands.

The king was seated on a carved wooden throne atop a small raised dais. Queen Laurel was seated to his left in a much plainer chair, and the king's advisor, Simon Pennyroyal, stood to his right. Ripplemintz had often complained that *he* should be standing there, as he was Muckwood's official wizard and in most kingdoms throughout the land that would make you the king's confidant and advisor, but King Mervyn didn't place a lot of faith in magic. He was a man of few words and many swords. Everything about him was sharp, from his short beard that tapered to a point to his raised eyebrows with their impossible angles.

Twig stopped where the herald told him to and stared down at the floor, not sure where to look. The herald, whose name was actually, oddly enough, Harold, gave an, "Ahem," and poked Twig with an elbow, perhaps a bit harder than he meant to or perhaps not.

"Twig, the wizard's apprentice," Harold the herald announced in a bored tone that said exactly what he thought of wizards and apprentices in general. He elbowed Twig sharply again, and finally Twig realized what he was trying to get him to do. He bowed low, the long sleeves of his new tunic swishing against the floor. He stayed down, not sure if he was supposed to keep bowing or stand back up, but the herald had retreated after naming him and was somewhere back by the door. A few of the ladies giggled.

"Simon, are you sure this is the one we've been hearing about?" said King Mervyn, as if Twig weren't, in fact, standing right there. "He's much smaller than I thought he'd be."

"Magic has no size, my Lord," said Pennyroyal. "At least, not to my knowledge. I understand Pyrite of Goldlocke to be quite short. He is rumoured to be half dwarf."

"Stand up, boy, and let me get a real look at you," said the king.

Twig stood. He felt a bit like a scrawny cow taken to market.

The king leaned forward and took a good long look at Twig, up and down – from the tips of his new boots to the top of his still unruly head of hair. He did not look impressed, and Twig wondered if he should have made his

new clothes even fancier. They'd felt quite swanky until he'd entered the throne room. *"Are* you half dwarf, boy?"

"No, sir, your majesty, sir," said Twig, and there were a few more peeps of laughter from the edge of the room.

The king sat back. He seemed disappointed, but Twig wasn't sure if that was a good thing or not. His father always said, the less your betters knew about you, the safer you were.

"Show the king some magic, boy. *If* you can," said Pennyroyal. He sounded deeply bored.

Twig had expected this request and, on his way to the throne room, had even thought about what to do: something magical, obviously, maybe a bit of conjuring or something, but nothing *too* impressive. Nothing to make the king take any serious notice of him.

But that had been before.

He raised his arms in the air and shouted out a bit of Elvish that he had once learned from a travelling minstrel who had stopped by the Thicket household on her way to the Eternal Forest to the north:

"Eftelsein tur sindriisin bwrar"

Which was roughly translatable as, *May I kindly use your toilet, good sir?* as he was sure they wouldn't know what it meant anyway.

"A dragon battle royale!" he whisper-spelled afterwards, and that was the real spell.

Sparks shot from his fingertips and music suddenly played from nowhere and everywhere at once. A small fire-breathing dragon leapt from one of the tapestries and did battle with a battalion of knights from another. Tiny licks of flame conjured from candle flame set fire to the knights one by one until the dragon was left victorious. It flew into the air and then vanished after one final tiny roar of conquest.

Queen Laurel clapped and the lords and ladies *ooohhhed* and *ahhhhed*. Twig bowed again, a little deeper this time. It wasn't actually that amazing of a magical feat; Ripplemintz could even have done it, though it would have taken him a much longer spell and some preparation ahead of time.

"Excellent!" said the king, sitting up straight. "Excellent. That will do nicely."

"Thank you, Your Majesty," said Twig, noticing that no one twittered this time.

"It's decided then," continued the king. "You'll be representing Muckwood in the Euphonium this year. Do us proud, boy. It's time for my kingdom to receive the recognition it deserves. You shall not disappoint us."

The way he said the last bit made it quite clear that disappointing the king was a course of action not to be recommended under any circumstances.

"Um . . ." began Twig.

"Yes, yes, I know, it's a great honour," said the king, waving a royal hand in the air. "I shall be sure to look after your family while you are away and they shall also be duly compensated . . . provided you are successful. I'm certain they are very proud, etc., etc."

"Er . . . " said Twig. He had the impression that *not* being victorious would bode ill for his many brothers and sisters. Was the king serious? Muckwood *never* competed in the Euphonium, at least not to his knowledge. Certainly never while Ripplemintz had

45

been the king's wizard.

"You may leave, boy," said Pennyroyal firmly. "Harold, bring in the next one, will you?" He turned to the king. "An open and shut case, your majesty. A brigand caught red-handed robbing a coach in the woods."

The king inclined his head in brief thought. "Off with his hands, then, no need to bring him in."

Twig backed quickly and silently out of the room and past the thief in question, who looked to be only a few years older than him. He'd never thought it would happen, but he agreed with his father about something. It *was* much safer if your betters didn't know who you were.

And much, *much* safer if they didn't send you off to the Euphonium. The Euphonium was a yearly gathering of wizards, witches and the like from all the known kingdoms. Except, of course, for those that dwelled in the Midden, which was just as well as no one generally liked to hang out with trolls, goblins and other creatures who might eat you as soon as look at you. The Euphonium was part carnival, part meeting ground, part marketplace, and, most importantly, a test of skill for those both willing and brave enough to take part. Or perhaps foolish was a better word. If you didn't die competing in the Euphonium, there was a good chance you'd leave it irrevocably changed, and not in a good way.

It was only a bit over one week away, and it took at least four days of non-magical travel to get there from Muckwood. That didn't leave much time for him to figure out how to rid himself of his curse and get back to normal, everyday boring Twig. The Twig that no one expected anything from.

5

IN WHICH THERE IS A HAG

Twig awoke the next morning with a headache from too little sleep and too much magic. He'd spent the remainder of the day before trading magic favours for coin (or cakes and sweets from Cook), conjuring up new unpickable locks for the windows in the tower (after Glimfinkle visited them again and wouldn't leave until they'd forcibly chucked him out the window – though Twig had conjured up a stiff breeze to make sure the gnome landed on his feet) and brainstorming with Ripplemintz on ways to rid himself of his problem. On the plus side, it was the best breakfast he'd ever eaten.

"I know what I'm going to do," said Twig, stabbing a bit of cake.

"Oh?" replied Ripplemintz.

"I'm going to go back to being me, like before."

"Oh?" said Ripplemintz again. He buttered a scone and then slathered it with jam. "And exactly how are you going to do that?"

"Well, I'm the world's most powerful wizard, right?"

"It would certainly appear so, but who am I to say? I haven't met all of the wizards in the world."

"Right," said Twig, ignoring that last bit. Ripplemintz *did* like to be precise, except when he didn't. "So I'm going to magic myself back to normal. Easy-peasy."

The sage dropped his scone jam-side down on to the table. "You mustn't do that."

"Why not?" said Twig. He'd even calculated in his head exactly how the spell might work.

"Taking someone's power, even your own, requires very, very strong magic," said Ripplemintz. "It is, let's face it, a bit of a dark art. We're talking Nix's Unravelling, like what Sumac used on his nan. Good wizards just don't *do* that. And besides, what happens in the middle of the spell when it starts to take effect and suddenly you don't have the power any more to finish it?"

Twig hadn't thought of that. "Er ... what do you think would happen?"

"I don't know," said Ripplemintz simply.

"But it *could* work," said Twig stubbornly.

"Perhaps," said Ripplemintz. "Or perhaps you'll blow yourself up. Or worse."

"What's worse than blowing yourself up?"

Ripplemintz stared at him. "Did you really mean to say that?"

Twig gulped. "No," he said. "Forget I said that." He took a pinch of salt and threw it over his shoulder and then knocked on the wood table for good measure. Words had power, after all.

"And," said Ripplemintz, "if what you've done is make yourself, essentially, into a containment vessel ... Tell me, Twig, how many times have you had to sweep up broken glass from this tower when a spell went wrong and things got out of hand?"

"A lot," said Twig. He didn't mention that the reason was usually because of how bad Ripplemintz was at spells. Now didn't seem like the time. But he had to admit to himself that, even if he *did* feel all-powerful, he still didn't know much about magic or the extent of his newfound abilities. He'd only been Ripplemintz's apprentice for a year, and certainly the old wizard hadn't taught him all that much, other than how to clean up broken things.

"I rest my case," said Ripplemintz. "We might be able to come up with a solution to your problem, but it will take a great deal of research."

He rubbed his hands together gleefully, a smile peeking out from his beard. "Years of research, even! No one has ever had a problem like this before!"

Twig pushed his breakfast away. That certainly wasn't going to help him get out of the Euphonium. Ripplemintz's accidental spell had turned into one humungous curse as far as he was concerned. And curses weren't wizard-work. They were the specialty of the hag, and the uglier, the better.

*

Twig knew exactly where the hag of Muckwood lived because his mum had often threatened to send him there. The rundown little hut was on the very outskirts of town, in between the tanner (whom no one wanted to live near) and the edge of the Withering Swamp that helped give Muckwood its name.

Twig held his nose past the tanner's house and walked right up to the door of the hag's hut. Well, it wasn't so much a door as it was a leftover length of tanned troll skin that the tanner hadn't wanted (you never could completely get rid of the smell). And it wasn't so much a house as it was a pile of sticks held together by things that didn't really bear looking at. There wasn't anywhere to knock, and nothing so fancy as a bell to ring, so Twig simply pulled back the greenish troll skin and went inside.

"Hello? Is the hag in?" he said into the gloom inside. The morning sun was out in full force but between the moss-draped trees that towered above the little hut and the fact that it had no windows at all (only spots where the sticks didn't quite go together), the inside of the hut seemed as dark as the inside of a troll. It smelled like it too.

A single candle sputtered into light, making Twig blink. The first thing he noticed was the hag's hand hovering over the flame. Her fingernails were pointed and slightly green. The arm attached to the hand was scrawny and covered in greenish brownish blobs that looked a bit like warts but even more like the kind of mushrooms his dad had warned him against picking. A tattered, filthy shawl hung around her hunched shoulders and head, leaving only a small opening through which a large fleshy hooked nose stuck out. It quivered as she inclined her head at him.

"Come in, come in," the hag growled. She had a voice like rocks rubbing together. She coughed and waved him in. "Someone you want cursed?" she cackled, and coughed again. He hoped she didn't have anything he could catch.

Twig stepped carefully inside, letting the troll skin fall back into place heavily behind him. Immediately the air inside the hut seemed to go completely still and stuffy and unbearably stinky. The hag pointed him to a small dirty cushion on the

floor, much like the one she was sitting cross-legged on herself. The hut was improbably tiny. How in the world did anyone live in something so small and filthy? He sat down, trying very hard not to touch anything at all.

"A pox on someone, then, dearie?" said the hag. "Someone done you wrong?" Her words ground together, going up and down the scale, like when his brother Badger's voice had changed when he hit puberty. "What's your name, then, young man?"

"Twig," he said. "I don't want a pox or a curse or anything like that. I want to see about how to remove one." Then he thought perhaps he'd better be polite, as she was a hag after all and seemed awfully anxious to curse someone. He held out his hand. "Nice to meet you. What's your name?"

The hag seemed surprised, though it was hard to tell when he couldn't see her eyes or much of her face other than the nose that seemed to have a life of its own. She took his hand and shook it. "You can call me Vile," she said.

"Your parents named you Vile?" he asked in surprise before he thought better of it. It did seem a very good name for a hag, but he was almost sure hags were taught, not born.

She pulled her hand back. "Your parents named you Twig?" she said shortly, in a tone that did not invite further questions. She coughed again. "So, tell me about this curse you wish removed."

"It's a bit hard to explain," he said, shifting on the lumpy cushion.

"Are you an elder son?"

"No."

"The middle child?"

"Not really."

"The youngest?"

"No. I'm kind of around the middle of twelve children."

"Cursed at birth?"

"No."

"Annoyed the fairies then, did you? Stumbled into a fairy mound when you weren't wanted? Stole some fairy bread?"

"No. Never really talked to any if I could help it."

"Ran afoul of a witch?"

"No."

"You're not a prince in disguise, surely?" The hag sounded a bit too dismissive for his taste, but he shook his head all the same. He certainly wasn't that. "Broke a mirror? Walked under a ladder? Crossed paths with a black cat? Spilled the salt cellar? Orphaned? Parents made a deal with a witch that went badly? Mum got a taste for cabbages from someone else's garden while pregnant with you?"

He'd never known his mum to touch a cabbage if she could help it. It gave her gas. "None of those," he said.

The hag sat back with a grumble. "Maybe we'd best start over. What exactly are you cursed with?" She leaned forward again and he could nearly feel her eyes burning through him. He imagined they were small and shrivelled like coals. "I don't see a tail or any boils or the usual. What is it you've got, exactly?"

"I'm the world's greatest wizard," he said miserably.

She didn't say anything for a moment. Then, finally:

"Get out," she said, and pointed at the door. "Did Pansy put you up to this?" Her voice, which had sounded so gravely and guttural before, now sounded a lot more like his older sister's. Petulant and annoyed. *Very* annoyed.

"I don't know who Pansy is," Twig said. "And I'm serious. Watch." He threw his hands up in the air. *"Let there be light!"* he proclaimed, perhaps more grandly than was necessary. The single candle multiplied into five, then ten, then twenty, each one floating up to hang in the still air of the hut.

For the first time in perhaps ever, the inside of the

hut was completely illuminated. Now he could see under the shawl and make out the hag's face clearly.

"Hey!" he yelled. "You're not a hag at all!" He reached out without thinking and pulled the nose off of the girl's face. It was actually a rotting parsnip. The hag looked to be around his age with sparkling green eyes that didn't at all resemble the empty coal-coloured sockets he had imagined.

Vile snatched the parsnip back. "Yes, I am too a hag!"

"But you're, like, eleven! And pretty!" The warts didn't just *look* like mushrooms; they *were* mushrooms, stuck on with some dried porridge.

"I'm *twelve*!"

"Where's the real hag?" Twig demanded.

"I *am* the real hag," the girl said firmly. Then she started to cry, but in a very angry way.

Twig bit back what he'd been about to say. He sighed and patted the girl on the shoulder. She snarled at him and he snatched his hand away.

"What did your mum really name you?" he asked, trying to take her mind off crying.

"Viola," she sniffled.

"That's a pretty name," he said and patted her cautiously again.

"Shut up," she said, wiping away her tears with the filthy shawl and leaving a smear of dirt across her face. It fell back from her head to uncover hair the colour of sunsets and campfires that would have been beautiful if it hadn't been tangled in knots. "Hags aren't pretty."

She definitely wasn't like any of his sisters.

"OK then, Vile," he said, "how did you come to be the hag? I thought she was supposed to be a hundred years old or something like that."

"Agrimony is my great-aunt. I came to study with her a few months ago, to learn the business." Her tears had stopped and just the anger part was left.

Now they were getting somewhere.

"So, where's she at? Can I talk to her?" asked Twig. Vile glared at him, and even though her eyes weren't coal-like, they certainly did burn. "Not that you're not a great hag and all, but my problem is probably a problem for an, um, more experienced hag ..." he added, his words trailing off into silence.

Vile narrowed her eyes at him. "How exactly is being the 'world's greatest wizard' a problem, anyway? That's the stupidest thing I've ever heard."

"It *is* a curse, believe me. It has only been a few days and now the king wants me to compete in the Euphonium. So, if there's any way I could talk to your great-aunt – for instance, maybe right now – that would be great."

"I don't know where she is," said Vile.

"Did she go out for bread or . . . more mushrooms? When will she be back?"

Vile stood up, quivering with anger or perhaps something else. Twig wasn't sure what. "I don't know," she said. "What don't you understand about that? She said she needed something and she'd be right back and" – Vile's eyes were dangerously bright again – "that was over a month ago, and I DON'T KNOW WHERE SHE IS OR WHEN SHE'S COMING BACK!"

Twig stood up too and took a look around the dismal little hut. In his experience, people who hadn't been heard from in over a week tended to not *ever* be heard from again. It was one of the dangers of living in Muckwood. There was the Withering Swamp to one side and Rot Bog to the other, the Eternal Forest above and Marsh Hallow below, and then the Midden beyond that. Muckwood was more or less a precariously positioned island in the middle of a very nasty and dangerous sea, if that sea was mostly mire and was filled with the kind of fish that had teeth, will-o'-the-wisps and swamp gas.

"You've been living here all by yourself?" he said softly.

"It's not that bad," she sniffed.

"Well, why don't you come back to the castle with me? Maybe Ripplemintz will have some idea where your great-aunt has gone. He is the sage, after all."

"I don't know ..." said Vile. "What if another client comes?"

Twig looked at her. She looked awfully scrawny. "We've got food," he said.

Vile squared her shoulders. "Why didn't you say so to begin with? Let's go."

6

IN WHICH VILE HAS AN IDEA

Ripplemintz fed Vile, but only after insisting she take a bath. She'd had two baths, actually, as Ripplemintz had changed the water once it had turned brown and begun smelling like mushroom soup. Her hair was still knotted and tangled but looked much shinier than it had before. Twig didn't blame him. He'd thought the smell only came from the hut, but it clearly didn't. The sage wasn't any help with Vile's aunt Agrimony, however. They'd had a bit of a falling out over some spoiled toad warts and hadn't talked in quite some time.

"So, why exactly do you want to get rid of this curse

that's not a curse?" asked Vile once she had gobbled up half a chicken.

"The king says I have to represent Muckwood in the Euphonium," said Twig glumly.

"*Hmmmpph*," said Ripplemintz. "He's never asked *me* to do that." He sounded slightly insulted. "Of course, *I* like to keep all my fingers and toes about me."

"He didn't so much *ask*," said Twig. "But if I can figure out how to get rid of this curse before then, maybe I won't have to do it."

"You're the most powerful wizard ever." Vile rolled her eyes. "Why in the deep sea do you keep calling it a curse?" She was gnawing on the last chicken drumstick. There wasn't much left on the bone to chew, but she was giving it a good go. Her teeth had bits of chicken and veg stuck in them.

"I like my fingers and toes attached as much as the next person, thank you very much. And I definitely don't want to duel a bunch of power-hungry wizards for the glory of Muckwood." He glumly picked up a spoon and poked at the almost-empty platter. Vile had eaten most of it in very short order. All that was left was a parsnip and he suspected it was the one that had formerly been her nose.

There was a grumble of many voices outside the door and then a sharp rap as something solid thunked against it.

"Read the sign!" yelled Ripplemintz. "We're not open yet."

The sage had recommended that they (meaning Twig) hold standard hours to cut down on the number of visitors, though it hadn't seemed to dissuade people from showing up and queuing.

There was a sizzling sound and a great rush of air, and the door flew open with a bang that was felt even by the rats that dwelled at the bottom of the tower. A very wizardly-looking wizard stood in the doorway gripping an ebony-tipped staff. He was dressed all in black and wore a very tall, very pointed hat. But the first thing everyone noticed about him was the extremely large, purplish pus-filled boil on the end of his nose. There were more pustules covering his face and hands, but it was the one on the end of his nose that you couldn't help staring at, as it was so enormous it seemed that it might jump off and walk around on its own at any time. It jiggled in a most disturbing way.

"*Wooo*," whistled Vile, "you must've got on the wrong side of a hag, that's for sure!"

"Hello, Sumac," said Ripplemintz mildly, setting upright a goblet that had fallen over in the rush of air. "And to what do we owe the pleasure of your visit?"

Sumac Crabapple was one of those people that had always been ugly on the inside, but it had been his nan's dying curse that had brought the ugliness out for the world to see. Henbit Crabapple had been so ancient she couldn't even remember how old she was when her grandson had cast Nix's Unravelling on her to steal her power. Sumac's reasoning was that she was so old she certainly didn't need it any more.

But he hadn't counted on Henbit's highly developed sense of revenge and self-preservation. She was, after all, a ten-time winner of the hagging competition at the Euphonium and an expert on all things pus-filled. She died with a smile on her face. Sumac had been her least favourite grandchild.

"I've come to see the new upstart wizard for myself," Sumac said. "Where is he?"

Vile pointed at Twig. "Here you go," she said cheerfully.

Sumac swept forwards and pushed his face close to Twig's, a bit like a chicken inspecting something to see if it was edible or not. Twig tried very hard not to stare at the jelly-like wobble of the boil right in front of him, but he couldn't quite manage it. He backed away without even meaning to, afraid it was going to explode on him.

"*Hmmphf,*" said Sumac. "Doesn't look like much."

"Prettier than you," said Vile.

Sumac's face flamed red and then nearly purple, the boil practically pulsating with barely contained anger. "You dare . . . !" he said, pointing a long, twisted finger at her.

Twig could feel the wizard working up a spell. It felt dark and cruel and not at all how Ripplemintz's wizardly experiments felt. Ripplemintz wasn't called the sage for nothing; he was more excited about studying the effects of magic than actually doing it, which was probably why the spells he did generally blew up. At any rate, his magic felt rather soft and dusty and smelled of old paper, like a light breeze blowing through a library. Sumac's magic, on the other hand, was full of spite and gave off a slight odour of brimstone.

Vile felt it too. She knew a curse when she saw one and Sumac's magic was tinged with his nan's power. She stood up, making a warding symbol with one hand while holding a blunt and mostly useless kitchen knife in the other.

Ripplemintz, having had a lot of practice at getting out of the way of things about to go badly wrong, ducked under the table.

In hindsight, Twig realized later that he probably should have thrown up some kind of magical shield or even turned the nasty wizard into a toad to teach him a lesson. Instead, he panicked, yelled out a garbled "No!" and whacked the wizard on the nose with the spoon he was still holding.

Sumac's boil did what it had been threatening to do for years. It burst. Spectacularly. Putrid-smelling goo went everywhere, mostly on to the wizard's face but also onto Twig and whatever else was in the way. The spell he'd been about to cast fizzled and died.

There was a drippy silence as Sumac stared at Twig for a long moment.

"You will pay for that," he said as he spat out a bit of something Twig didn't want to think about.

"You can have it back," said Vile as she cast a hex on the angry wizard, and a big, disgusting boil immediately appeared back on his nose, along with some other new ones on his ears.

Sumac glared at them both. "We *will* meet again at the Euphonium." And with that dire pronouncement, he swirled around, his robes and cape twirling and twisting into a whirlwind. He blew out the door and down the stairs like an angry black cloud of wasps.

Ripplemintz climbed out from under the table and

the three of them stared out the door, which had been open the entire time. Only Cook was left standing there. "I'll, er, come back later," she said. "You can keep the cake." She set it down, what there was left of it, and scuttled off down the stairs. Much of the frosting had been blown into her hair.

Twig wiped his face with a bit of his sleeve and sat down.

"I guess you've made your point," said Vile.

"I have?" said Twig. He wasn't sure what she meant.

"Yeah, my mum always said wizards are a competitive bunch, every one wanting to be better than the next, and all that rot." She jerked a thumb towards the door. "He's probably just the first one." She clapped Twig on the back. It squelched wetly. "They're gonna try to absolutely murder you at the Euphonium, if not before. I sure am glad I'm not you."

"Thanks for that," he said.

"Well, my mum also always said that it takes a witch to fix a wizard's mess. *Everyone* knows that. So, if you really want to get rid of your power, it's

Witch Wormwood

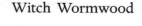

you should be asking."

"*Excellent* idea," said Ripplemintz. "You ought to go immediately . . . or right after you clean up this mess. And take Vile with you. Besides, if anyone will know where Agrimony has got herself off to, it will be that nosy old witch."

Witch Wormwood lived between the Withering Swamp and Marsh Hallow, which was a long walk from Muckwood, mostly because you had to go through a lot of mud, sludge and even slime to get there. Clever travellers took more than one pair of boots with them. Even cleverer ones didn't go at all.

Where hags specialized in curses, hexes and the like, witches were more generalized, as were wizards. The main difference between witches and wizards was that witches worked with nature, while wizards tended to try to control nature in any way they could. Plus, witches made do with whatever they had to hand, whereas wizards preferred flashy, expensive equipment, even if they didn't really need it. That was why wizards usually worked for royalty or rich landowners who could afford to pay them handsomely. Witches didn't work for anyone unless they wanted to.

Ripplemintz handed Twig a small sack. "Just in case you need it," he said. "You can't make magic out of nothing, remember. Not even you."

"Thanks," said Twig. He hefted the sack. It wasn't large or particularly heavy, but it did at least make him feel a bit better about Ripplemintz not having helped clean up the tower. He'd wondered what the old sage was pottering around doing while he and Vile had been busy, and now he knew.

Cleaning up the remains of Sumac's boil had been a thoroughly nasty job. He'd had to take a bath afterwards and even Vile had done the same, after complaining loudly that she'd had more baths in one day than she usually had in a month. Twig still didn't feel he'd quite been able to get rid of the odour. It lingered in his hair. It was like a cross between rancid milk and the smell of his brother Badger's shoes in summer. Sumac's nan must have been one mean but talented hag. He'd changed into travelling clothes for the extra pockets and thrown away the outfit he'd worn to see the king.

"Aren't you coming with us?" Vile asked Ripplemintz.

"Me?" The sage looked completely taken aback by the idea. "Of course not. I have three experiments running right now. I'm sure you two can take care of yourselves. Go on, then."

Twig shrugged at Vile. He hadn't expected Ripplemintz to come anyway. He never cleaned up his own messes so he certainly didn't expect him to help clean up a mess that he probably considered to be Twig's, though technically, wasn't this all really Ripplemintz's fault? After all, it had been *his* escaped accidental spell to begin with. None of this would have happened if he hadn't broken the bottle or if he hadn't been a braggart when he was young.

Twig and Vile headed down the steps. They had barely gone through the door when Twig felt something small but solid land on his shoulder.

"Bloomin' wizards," said a tiny voice. "Never no help, are they? Not ye, of course."

Twig sighed. "What do you want, Glimfinkle? I've already told you no a bunch of times."

Vile, who had been a few steps ahead, stopped and turned around at Twig's words. "What did you—" she started to say and then she got a glimpse of Glimfinkle. "Gah!" she yelled and swatted at the gnome. "There's a gnome! You've got a gnome on you!"

Twig dodged her flailing hands as Glimfinkle grabbed on to his hair and swung around to cling behind his neck, hollering the whole while in gnomish things that were probably not all that complimentary to Vile or hags in general.

"Control yer wee hag, would ye?" yelled Glimfinkle.

"She's not *my* hag," said Twig. But he did mutter a quick protection spell so that Vile's blows just glanced off of him. "Vile. VILE. It's JUST A GNOME. You can calm down now."

Vile stopped hitting him, which was an improvement, but continued to glare at him, which wasn't. "I don't like gnomes," she said.

"Well, I'm not that fond o' hags," said Glimfinkle, still hiding behind Twig's ear, "but ye don't see me tryin' ta bash yer brains in, do ye?"

"Like you could," she said, fingers out like she was about to cast a curse at him.

"Hang on!" said Twig. "No one's bashing anyone's brains out or cursing them or anything." He glared at Vile until she lowered her hand. "Now, Glimfinkle, what is it you want now?"

"Me? I wants to help ye," said the gnome.

Vile snorted. Twig ignored her and so did Glimfinkle.

"I don't think there's anything you can do, Glimfinkle, but thanks. We've really got to be going. I don't have time to stand here and argue with you."

It was Glimfinkle's turn to snort. "Ye think that witch in the swamp is goin' ta help ye? Witches are just as bad as wizards. The only one what's worse is a hag." He made some intricate symbol with his hands and then spit, which happily landed on the inside of the shielding spell and not on Twig or Vile. It hung there glistening wetly in the air.

"You little—!" began Vile, but Twig shot her another warning look and she actually subsided a little, rather like a pot taken off the fire just in time to keep it from boiling over. Maybe it was because he hadn't released the shield spell yet and she knew there wasn't anything she could do. A corner of his mind wondered how much energy it would take to keep the spell going permanently.

"Witch Wormwood might not help, but I have to try," said Twig. "It's the only plan I've got at the moment."

"That's what I'm tryin' to tell ye," said the gnome. "Ye don't need no witch. What ye need is a visit to the oracle."

"I don't know," said Twig. "The oracle's really far and I don't have much time. If Witch Wormwood can help, I can be back home before dinner tomorrow."

"That's where I come in, y'see," said Glimfinkle. "I know a shortcut. I can get ye there in three shakes."

"Out of the goodness of your tiny little heart," said Vile.

"O' course! O' course," said the gnome. He patted Twig on the cheek. "But if ye'd be wanting to do old Glimfinkle a favour or two after, I certainly wouldn't turn it down. A trade, if ye will. Quid pro quo."

Twig
sighed
again. He
plucked
Glimfinkle
off his shoulder
and put him down on a step.
"I'm sorry, Glimfinkle, but I don't have time for this.
I've got to get to Witch Wormwood. But thanks for
your offer of help." He hitched his head at Vile. "Let's
get going, we've wasted enough time already." He
started down the stairs, Vile clomping after him.

"Hey! Hey!" yelled the gnome. "The least ye could
do is get me to the bottom of the tower! Do you know
how long it took me to get up here?!"

"Allow me," said Vile with an evil grin.

"Eh, no, never ye mind," said the gnome. "Begone,
nasty hag."

"That's my sister," she said. "I'm Vile."

"That ye are," grumbled the gnome, staring after them. "That ye are."

Glimfinkle waited until they were out of sight and then put two fingers in his mouth, whistling one quick, sharp blast followed by a trill. A moment later, his magpie landed next to him.

The gnome patted the bird on the head and then climbed aboard. "He'll come to reason, Beaky," he said, half to himself, "He may be stubborn beyond all reason, but I do knows how to be *in-dee-spens-ible*. Let's go see Witch Wormwood. Gee yup!" And off they flew towards the swamp, passing over Twig and Vile before they had even left the castle grounds.

7

IN WHICH SOMEONE IS LOST

"So, you said you have a sister?" asked Twig as they walked the path that led past Vile's hag hut and into the swamp.

"Yes," said Vile. She clomped as she walked. Ripplemintz had given her an old pair of boots as well as a robe he had outgrown many years before. Both were too big for her. She had tied a bit of twine around her waist to pull in the robe, but it still billowed about her like she was wearing a tent. It was also a hideously horrible shade of puce with green stars. Twig had offered to magic it into something better or at least something that fit, but she had refused.

"How many?"

"Just one. A sister. Nasty."

"Her name is Nasty?" She hadn't been joking earlier. He wasn't sure why he was surprised. Of course Vile's sister was called Nasty.

Vile looked at him sideways. "Mum named her Nasturtium," she said finally, "but that's an even worse name for a hag than Viola is."

"Er, right," said Twig. "So, you're Nasty and Vile, then."

"Yes," she said proudly. "Nasty's older than me. She's working as a hag up in Aramore."

Aramore was the kingdom that hosted the Euphonium every year, it being the richest of all the kingdoms and the one with the most land. Aramore ran all the way from the edge of the Deep Sea though the plains and all the way to the bottom of the Falling Mountains. If Nasty was employed there, she was obviously pretty good at hagging.

Twig stayed silent for a while and concentrated on not falling over, using a sturdy stick he'd found for balance. They had entered the Withering Swamp, and the path was both bumpy and filled with holes. Dusk had started to fall and the air was filled with the sounds of birds and bugs and mysterious splashes that made you think of things creeping up on you. Twig didn't like the swamp. He liked solid ground and trees that stayed where they were supposed to.

"So . . . how did you and Nasty wind up as hags?"

"Dad's from a long line of hags. The Hornworts. You've probably heard of us?" Twig nodded even though he'd never heard the name before. If Ripplemintz had ever mentioned hags to him, he certainly didn't remember. "He'd have been one too, if he'd been born a girl. Granny Scab was very disappointed, you know, but then Nasty came along. She's a born hag, Nasty is."

Twig wasn't sure what that meant, but it didn't sound very nice to him. "And you too?" he said, hoping she'd keep talking. His boots were starting to stick with each step and he didn't want to think about what they were walking in. People said the Withering Swamp had been created from the decomposing bodies of the victims of the last great war between the goblins and the trolls. It certainly smelled like it.

But that seemed to have been the wrong question. Vile glared at him like he'd called her troll dung and then squelched ahead.

"Sorry," he said, though he wasn't sure what he'd done, and hurried to catch up to her. They walked on in silence, the air growing heavier and damper, almost like they were walking into a wet blanket. The few scraggly trees along the path were draped in moss and loomed over them like skinny, hairy giants. The path, or what there was of one, meandered close to the trees, probably because the rest of the ground had shifted too much. He saw a bobble of light floating off to their right and then it was gone again.

Ignis fatuus. Foolish fire. At least he had learned *something* from Ripplemintz. Never trust a will-o'-the-wisp. Don't be led astray. He resolutely looked away from the happily dancing dots of light that beckoned to him and focused on Vile's back, hoping she really did know where they were going.

"What about you?" she said out of nowhere.

"What about me?"

"How'd you wind up apprenticed to that wizard?"

"Oh." It wasn't really a very interesting story. No one else had wanted the job after the last two apprentices had not very mysteriously been blown up. "It was better than staying at home and living off of acorn stew."

"Oh," said Vile. "Yeah, you were one of twelve, right?"

He was surprised that she remembered. "Yes. Sort of in the middle. My oldest brother is twenty-four and the youngest is two. Six boys and six girls." He tried to think of something else interesting to say about his family but couldn't think of anything that anyone would want to know.

There was a rattling sound that echoed around for a moment and then stopped, and Twig saw three more small balls of light bouncing here and there in the inky, misty gloom that surrounded them.

Vile stopped so suddenly that Twig nearly ran into her back. "Do you think you could magic up a light? My hag sense is telling me there's something out there."

Twig had never heard of "hag sense", but he held his

walking stick aloft.

"*Light, bright, take back the night,*" he said, rather pleased with himself at the quick rhyme. Spells always held better when they rhymed.

A blazing bluish glow lit up the branch, making it look a bit like he was holding aloft a glimmering skeletal arm. To the right of the trail, quite near them and blinking in the sudden light, was something shaped vaguely like a small, hunched over man with stringy greenish-grey hair. He stood in murky water reaching up to his knees, and wore a coat with layers and layers of shells sewn on to it that rattled as he twitched backwards in the light. There were tears running down his gaunt face.

"*Hsssshht!*" hissed Vile and made the sign of the evil eye at the creature. "Begone!"

"But I'm *lost!*" wailed the little man, his shells clacking.

"We're not falling for that old trick," said Vile firmly. "Now leave this place and go back whence you came."

Twig moved closer to Vile. "What *is* he?" he whispered.

"Shellycoat," she whispered back. "Don't trust him. They're as bad as will-o'-the-wisps, though they won't kill you on purpose. Just laugh their heads off once they've tricked you."

The little man sniffled and wiped at his eyes with the back of his hand. He didn't look like he had *ever* laughed.

"Though ..." said Vile thoughtfully, "you don't normally see them in swamps. And usually they're pretending to drown so that you'll try and save them. But maybe this one has learned some new tricks."

A few will-o'-the-wisps floated up and the little man swatted at them in between his sobs. He took a step to the left and then turned around and took a few steps back the other direction. His coat of shells clicked and clacked.

"Come on," said Vile, "ignore him." She squelched off along the path.

"Are you *really* lost?" Twig asked the shellycoat.

"Yes, master, *yes*," the little man wailed, louder than before. He sloshed towards Twig,

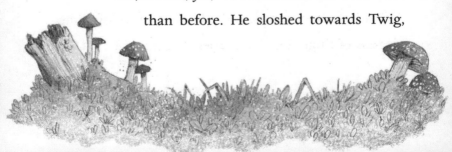

hands out. His skin was grey and he had warts all over him. In fact, even his warts had warts.

"Twig!" yelled Vile. "What are you *doing*?"

"I think he's actually lost," said Twig.

"You're an idiot," said Vile.

Twig stared at the little man. He was shorter than Twig, only coming up a bit above his waist, and he smelled like the inside of a conch seashell that a peddler had once brought to Muckwood. Twig wondered whether the little man would sound like the waves if you put your ear to him, like the shell had.

"Where do you live?" asked Twig.

"Along the Witch Fingers, master. I was looking for a new shell for my coat and there was a lovely one, there was, being carried in the current. I followed the water. But now ..." His long, grey fingers fiddled with an empty spot on his sleeve where a shell must have fallen off. "The water here is tasteless," he said and sniffled again.

"You're quite a ways from home," said Twig. The Witch Fingers was where the Endless River split into dozens of finger-like tributaries that stretched all the way to the Deep Sea. The water in much of it was brackish and salty. One of those tributaries flowed into the swamp, but he had no idea how to find it. "That's due west from here, maybe a day and a half's walk."

Vile blew a raspberry with her lips. "Twig, we're wasting what little light is left," she said. "We've still got an hour's travel *at least* until we get to Witch Wormwood's."

Twig didn't answer. He knew she was technically right, but he couldn't bring himself to leave the little crying man. He unslung Ripplemintz's sack from his shoulder. Maybe there would be something helpful in it? Handing the still-flaming branch to Vile, who took it gingerly, Twig opened the sack and rummaged through it to find anything useful. Some stale bread. A spool of thread. A shiny black lump of stone. A few rusty iron nails. A bag of sugar cubes, the kind that pixies liked best. A teacup with a chipped edge. A broken mousetrap with a mouse stuck in it that was so long-dead that it had dried out. He nearly dropped that on the ground when he pulled it out, but he stuck his hand back in anyway. It looked like Ripplemintz had merely thrown a bunch of rubbish in the sack, though surely he must have put *something* useful in there.

"Ow!" Twig said as something poked him. He pulled out his hand to find a needle embedded in his thumb. He yanked it out and sucked the pinprick of blood away.

"Time is ticking," said Vile. "*Tick, tick, tick.*"

An inkling of an idea came to Twig. "Hold on a minute," he said, as he fished out the teacup and the black stone. The little man stared up at him hopefully but mournfully.

Twig had seen the black stone before – Ripplemintz used it in some of his spells, mostly the ones to do with weather and locating things. It was a lodestone. He rubbed the needle on it a few times.

"Master is very clever," said the Shellycoat, sounding doubtful.

"You don't need to call me that," said Twig. "I'm not your master. I'm no one's master. My name's Twig."

"Thank you, Master Twig."

Twig sighed. Using the teacup, he scooped up some water from a relatively muck-free spot in the swamp and looked around for the last bit of what he needed.

"Vile," he said. "Can you come here a minute?"

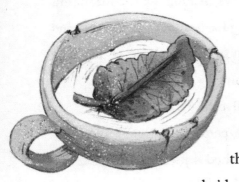

Vile sloshed over, looking curious despite herself. Twig picked a small beech tree leaf out of her hair. She *had* been mostly clean when they'd left the tower, but she'd already started building a new layer of dirt and debris. As far as he could tell, she *was* a born hag like her sister. She just didn't have any warts.

"Thanks," he said.

He carefully set the leaf on top of the water in the teacup and then very, very gently set the needle on top of the leaf. He held his breath as it slowly swirled around and then stopped. He turned the cup this way and that and watched the leaf rotate inside the cup, the tip of it always pointing the same way. It worked!

"What strange magic is this?" asked the Shellycoat.

"It's not magic at all, really," said Twig, though in

a way it was, as he couldn't remember exactly how lodestones worked. "I've made you a compass. Hold the cup this way," he said as he held out the teacup for the shellycoat to take. "The leaf with the needle always points north. Now, all you've got to do is always walk to the *left* of where it's pointing. That's west."

"Left?" asked the Shellycoat.

"This side," said Twig, patting the little man on his left arm. "Always go that way. If you do that, you'll end up in the right place. You can find your way home once you get back to the Witch Fingers, right?"

"Oh, yes, master!"

The Shellycoat darted off a few steps (happily, in the correct direction), with the handle of the cup gripped tightly in one hand. Then he dashed back. "Master Twig has been very kind," he said. He dug into a pocket of his rattling coat and pulled out a small bag. "For you, master!" And then he darted off again.

Twig peeked into the pouch. It was full of seashells of every description and colour. He put it in Ripplemintz's sack, along with the lodestone.

"You're a weird one," said Vile. "Why didn't you

magic something up instead?"

"Because," said Twig stiffly, taking back his walking stuck and squelching off up the path. He was a little ashamed to admit that he hadn't even thought of using magic. After all, he'd only been the world's greatest wizard for a few days.

8

IN WHICH THERE IS A WITCH, WHICH WASN'T WHAT THEY WANTED

They hurried on, Vile taking the lead again once Twig realized it was silly for him to be in front when he had no idea where they were going. True to her word, they reached Witch Wormwood's house about an hour later, after leaving the path and splashing through knee-deep water to get to a roundish clearing with only a few small stunted trees in it. Twig's boots were completely full of water and things he didn't want to think about. Vile didn't seem to mind.

The witch's wooden house was perched precariously on stilts with stairs zig-zagging up one side. Smoke drifted from a crooked chimney, and the warm glow of a fire shone through the two square windows. It would have looked very cosy if it were located anywhere else.

"How do you know Witch Wormwood?" asked Twig. A few witches had come to do business with

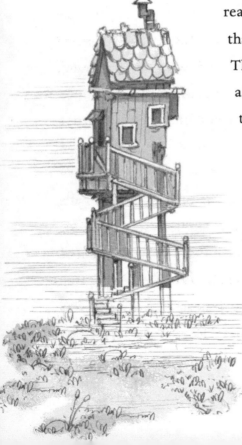

Ripplemintz, but he'd never really talked to any other than to offer them tea. They had all been at least as old as Ripplemintz and twice as crotchety.

"I don't," said Vile.

"Then how did you know how to get here?"

"My aunt Agrimony had me deliver things here a few times. Troll dung, rooster eyeballs, things like that. But Witch Wormwood was never home when I arrived, so I left the basket at the door. She travels a lot."

Twig looked at the house and the twist of smoke climbing from the chimney. After all their walking, at least it looked like someone was home. They climbed up the stairs, and Twig was about to knock on the door when he thought about how rude it would be to enter a witch's house dripping water all over the floor.

"Wind and fire, water and air, make us fair," he whispered, and he held still as a warm breeze picked up from nowhere and spun them around, drying them off.

"Hey!" said Vile. "You could have warned me you were going to do that!"

"Sorry—"

The door flew open, cutting off Twig's apology. A skinny woman with a much smaller nose than Twig had imagined any witch having stood wild-eyed in the door, a broomstick held in her hands. She wasn't particularly hideous – or pretty, for that matter – and wore a simple green dress with loads of pockets. Her brown hair was streaked with silver and a single curl hung down right in the middle of her forehead.

"Who's that doing magic on my front porch?" she demanded, poking the business end of the broomstick towards them.

Twig stared. *This* was a witch? She looked almost normal. "Sorry," Twig said again. "I was trying to dry us off before we knocked, so we wouldn't get your house all wet." He attempted a smile.

"And *who* might *you* be?" Witch Wormwood peered at him through narrowed eyes. Her eyebrows were quite serious.

"I'm Twig," he said. "I'm Ripplemintz's apprentice. I think you—"

"And you?" the witch said, interrupting him and piercing Vile with her pointed glare.

"Vile. Agrimony is my—"

"You're late," Witch Wormwood said abruptly, lowering the broomstick. "Come in. Leave your boots outside. There's bound to be something hiding in them." She turned around and went back in, leaving the door open.

Twig and Vile looked at each other and dutifully added their boots to the line-up of shoes along the edge of the porch along the wall. The witch had three pairs of identical clunky black boots already lined up. A frog jumped out of one of them as they set theirs down, and jumped off the edge of the porch, landing with a splash and a croak in the water below.

They went inside. The witch sat in a wooden rocking chair in front of a cheerful fire, legs stretched out to the blaze, wiggling her toes at the flames. She was wearing stripy socks. Glimfinkle the gnome was perched on a tufted footstool at her feet, drinking from a tiny mug of tea.

"That stupid gnome is here," said Vile darkly.

"What are *you* doing here?" Twig asked Glimfinkle.

"Waitin' on ye," the gnome said. "What took ye so long?" He took a dainty sip of tea. "I've already explained yer little predicament to Wormwood. We go way back. Come on, then, don't just stand there. Sit down. There's chairs enough."

And there were. Two straight-backed chairs were pulled up to the fire waiting for them. Witch

Wormwood pointed to a tray of biscuits and tea on a small table between them. They took a cup and a biscuit each. Vile shoved the whole biscuit into her mouth at once and reached for another.

"Er . . ." began Twig.

"Can't help you," said Witch Wormwood. "I'm surprised Ripplemintz didn't tell you that himself. The old coot should know better." She gave a nod to Glimfinkle, who nodded back with an *I-told-ye-so* expression on his face.

"Can't or won't?" asked Vile around a mouthful of crumbs.

"Both," said the witch.

"Why not?" asked Twig. How could it be both? If

she couldn't, that was one thing, but if she could but just wouldn't, what possible reason could there be?

"Haven't you read any books, boy? This is the kind of problem you've got to solve for yourself." She rocked herself back and forth in her chair. "Any fool knows that. Not even the People's Wizard could help you with this, if he's even still alive." She nodded at Glimfinkle again. "Even wee little *gnomes* know that."

"Hey, now," said Glimfinkle, sitting up as tall as he could. "No need to get personal."

"Though," continued the witch, "you are a bit young to be cursed like—"

"He's precocious!" interrupted the gnome. "And it's not like it's his fault, ye know."

At least the gnome was standing up for him.

"I've got coin, if that's what you're after," Twig said. He'd actually managed to collect a decent amount of money doing magic for people in a short amount of time. Certainly more than he'd ever had in his life before. More than he'd ever *seen* in all his life, actually. He'd brought it all with him.

"Doesn't matter," said the witch. "Better

eat your biscuit, but don't forget to brush your teeth. *Very* important in your situation." The witch winked at him.

"Eat up!" said Glimfinkle. He looked entirely too happy.

Twig was silent. He bit into his biscuit and chewed thoughtfully. Did Witch Wormwood mean he had to solve it for himself because he'd caused the problem? It *had* been his containment spell that had trapped the spell inside him. So maybe he was the only one who could undo it? But Ripplemintz had said there was a good chance he'd blow himself up. If there was one thing the sage knew, it was how to blow things up. Twig took another bite of biscuit, not even tasting it.

"And you might want to brush your hair," said Witch Wormwood, still watching him over her teacup. "Best to keep yourself clean and in top shape, you know." She glanced at Vile and then back at him. "Well, usually. Maybe in your case it won't matter."

"Er, thanks, I guess," said Twig. The witch was full of advice, but it really didn't seem very useful.

Maybe Glimfinkle had been right and he should just go see the oracle.

Vile, in the meantime, had finished off the rest of the biscuits and her tea. She cleared her throat. "Witch Wormwood, have you seen Agrimony recently?" she asked.

"Gone off and left you to fend for yourself, did she?"

"No!" said Vile. "Well, maybe. I don't know."

"Always was a bit flighty," said Witch Wormwood, nodding. "Her curses didn't even stick half the time. I'd advise you to find yourself another hag to apprentice under."

Vile fidgeted on her seat. "She's my great aunt," she said.

"So? Nothing stopping you finding yourself a better hag to learn from. All the more reason, if you ask me."

"But I can't," said Vile miserably. She stared down at the rag rug on the floor. It looked like it was made of snakeskin and swamp grass.

"Why not?" asked Twig, drawn out of his own problem in spite of himself. What the witch had said made sense to him. After all, aunt or not, Agrimony had left without a word or anything. He knew first hand that just because someone was family, that didn't necessarily make them nice or responsible or kind. Relatives were accidents of fate.

"*Because*," said Vile.

Witch Wormwood cackled – a proper witchy cackle that made the hair on the back of Twig's neck stand on end – and leaned towards Vile. "Tell him why, dearie." She looked like *she* already knew somehow, but maybe that was a witch thing.

Vile scowled. "Because I'm not ugly enough," she said through gritted teeth. "No one else would have me. They all say I'm too *pretty*." She practically spat out the last word and shuddered at the same time.

Twig stared at her, not knowing what to say.

Witch Wormwood cackled again. "We are who we are, girlie girl," she said, "every one of us. Ever thought about being a witch? No one cares what you look like one way or another, so long as your spells work."

Twig opened his mouth and then promptly closed it again. He'd been about to say something extremely ill-advised about how he'd always thought witches were supposed to be nearly as ugly as hags, but he'd thought better of it and took a sip of tea instead.

"I'm a Hornwort," said Vile, lifting up her chin. "I'm a *hag*."

"Yeah, yeah, yer a lovely wee hag," interrupted Glimfinkle. "Now, are the two of ye ready to meet the oracle or what? *She's* the one ye need to talk to. Ye'll need a guide – I can take ye to her cave." He raised his tiny mug in Twig's direction in a small toast. To what, Twig wasn't sure.

"Will the oracle be able to help?" Twig said to Witch Wormwood and not the gnome. At least she seemed honest. Blunt, but honest.

The witch shrugged. "Doubtful, but it couldn't hurt."

"Of course she can help!" shouted Glimfinkle. "I swear by my Dah's beard!"

That didn't make Twig feel any better.

9

IN WHICH THERE ARE TWO PROBLEMS: ONE BIG, ONE SMALL

They stayed the night at Witch Wormwood's as it was too late and entirely too dark to walk back through the swamp without winding up victim to something incredibly mucky. Besides dodgy will-o'-the-wisps, the Withering Swamp was full of nuggies of every shape and size and green-toothed nixies that left behind nasty bites that had a tendency to get infected.

The witch even treated them to a dinner of frog stew followed by jelly. It was surprisingly good, if you didn't think too much about why everything was green. The same thing could be said about breakfast the next morning. Was it a witch thing or a swamp thing?

As they ate their greenish-blue pancakes and slightly purple sausages, Witch Wormwood passed a small bag of mints, a bar of soap, and a brush to Twig, as well as some food.

"Best to be prepared at all times," she said with a wink. Twig thanked her even though he wasn't sure what fresh breath and neat hair would do for him in the grand scheme of things.

"That's me motto!" said Glimfinkle, looking very pleased with himself. Twig had seen him roll up an extra pancake and stick it under his beard. Witch Wormwood pointedly pretended not to notice.

"I'll send a Pixie Post to Ripplemintz letting him know where you're off to," said Witch Wormwood, as she added another miniature pancake to Glimfinkle's plate.

"You've got Pixie Post here?" asked Vile.

"Well, I'm the closest thing to a village the Withering Swamp has," said the witch. "And I make up special dragonmint-flavoured sugar cubes for them."

"Thanks," said Twig. "Can you tell him we'll send

another message after we visit the oracle?" He hoped that one would contain better news.

"Do you even know how to get to the oracle?" asked Vile, poking a finger at the gnome.

That was a good question. Twig had never actually been much beyond Muckwood before. He'd ventured into the forest to forage, certainly, as all the children of the village did who couldn't afford not to. He had no idea how to get to where they needed to go.

"Of course I do!" said the gnome. "She lives in a cave by the Pool of Truth and Wisdom just over Vine Gorge. Here, I'll draw ye a map."

The gnome sketched out a quick map on a piece of parchment. After leaving the Withering Swamp, they would go through the Eternal Forest and then cross Vine Gorge. The oracle's cave was all the way up near the Spire Kingdom, home of Kudzu, the famed half-elf wizard.

"That looks like a long way," said Twig doubtfully.

"So 'tis," said Glimfinkle. "We'd best get to it!"

Glimfinkle and Beaky led the way, the magpie flying ahead

in short hops as Twig and Vile followed along. They made it out of the swamp and into the forest by noon, but it was slow going. By early evening they were still surrounded by trees with no end in sight. It wasn't called the Eternal Forest for nothing, Twig supposed.

"I'm starving and I'm tired," said Vile, stopping dead in her tracks. She flopped down on the ground and leaned back against a tree. "How much further, you lazy gnome?"

Beaky had been riding on Twig's shoulder with Glimfinkle on his back, but now he flew down next to Vile so that the gnome could climb off and stretch. "Don't expect we're gonna get there 'til after nightfall. Most like, it'll be morning."

Vile groaned.

"So's we should keep goin'," said Glimfinkle. "And ye talk about *me* bein' lazy . . ." He clucked his tongue.

"You're riding!" said Vile. "We're *walking*!"

"Let's just take a little break," said Twig. He was tired too, but he wasn't sure if he was more exhausted from all the walking or them sniping at each other all the time.

He took out some of the flat traveller's bread that Witch Wormwood had given them and split it between them. For a while, all was quiet and peaceful, partly because the bread was oddly chewy and had unidentifiable lumps in it. Twig decided not to think about what the lumps might be.

As they ate, the forest around them grew quieter until all Twig could hear was the sound of them eating. He finished his last bite and swallowed.

"Do you hear that?" he asked.

"Wot?" asked Glimfinkle.

". . . The *nothing*," said Vile. She looked at Twig and then around them. "You're right." She rubbed the back of her neck. "I guess I was too hungry to notice before, but my hag sense is tingling. I don't like it."

"Yer don't like anythin' so far as I can tell," grumbled the gnome, but he stood up and took a look around anyway, motioning to Beaky. The magpie flew up and circled above them twice before diving back down, squawking something as loud as he could, and then flying up, up and away.

"RUN!" yelled Glimfinkle, but it was already too

late. The silence was broken by a loud THUNK! as a nearby tree was shattered clean in half by a massive club. Splinters flew in every direction.

The green-skinned beast holding the club was appropriately sized for such a giant weapon. It was an ogre big enough to crush pretty much anything it wanted to. Two teeth stuck out of its mouth like oversized boar tusks and it had a single slightly off-centre horn on top of its head. It wore a bandolier of bones across its ridiculously muscular, battle-scarred chest and a ratty, moth-eaten pelt was tied around its waist almost like an afterthought.

It pushed through the remains of the tree it had just smashed and sniffed in their direction. Had it been tracking them?

It was the biggest, scariest thing Twig had *ever* seen.

Twig stood frozen, until Vile pulled him to his feet. Away they scrambled, and the ogre let out a roar so terrifying that Twig was fairly certain his heart actually stopped for a moment before thudding back into life. Branches slapped him in the face as they ran, but they didn't get far. Twig tripped over a tree root, taking Vile down with him and dropping his walking stick. It rolled away, useless.

"Git up," screamed Glimfinkle. "He's gonna smash yer brains in and then eat 'em!" He was already running towards a tiny gnome-sized hole at the base of a tree as fast as his little legs would take him.

"Fresh meat!" The ogre's deep, guttural voice almost gurgled. Was it *laughing* at them?

All Twig could think was that they had to get away, hide. But where? How? The club smashed into the tree right above them, making the whole thing shudder, all the way up to the very top. Twig rolled to the left, scraping against the rough bark. A jolt of pain shot down his arm. Leaves rained down on his head.

"Do something!" yelled Vile. "Use your magic!" She

was on her knees, tangled up in Ripplemintz's old robe and struggling to stand back up.

Twig went blank. This was it. They were ogre food. Spell? What spell? He couldn't think of a spell. All he could think was that he couldn't breathe. All he could hear was the creature's grating laughter *GRAHH HAH HA* and the *WHOOSH* of the club as it swished through the air. It was toying with them, like a cat playing with a mouse. Vile was screaming curses, but he didn't see how giving the beast boils was going to help. It was already the ugliest thing Twig had ever seen.

He scrabbled backwards and his hand caught in the hole the gnome had disappeared into. If only they could fit inside the hole too! What if—

"Small as a mouse!"

It was the first time he'd ever cast a transformation spell on himself, and too late he remembered Rippleminz's warning to always, *always* concentrate extra special hard when performing a spell like this. If your concentration

wavered even a bit, or your intent wasn't clear . . .

But the spell was already underway, and Twig felt himself shrinking. Next to him, Vile was shrinking too. Down, down, down they shrank – down to the size of a dog, then a cat, then a rabbit. The ogre, confused by their sudden change, raised his club far above their heads and brought it down with another blood-curdling bellow, obliterating the bush behind them, but it was too late. It missed them. Twig breathed a sigh of relief.

But as they shrank further still, brownish-grey fur began to sprout along their arms, and then everywhere else as well. Vile twisted about in surprise and Twig saw a tail peek out from underneath her robe. He could feel his own sprouting as well and let out an involuntary *eep!* as it poked through the back of his breeches. But even the shock of that squeezed out of his head as his nose began to lengthen and whiskers popped out one by one. As the spell finally spun itself out, Twig found himself down on all fours.

For a moment, he and Vile looked at each other in shock, but then they ran into the hole before the club hit the ground right where they had been, blocking out the light. As the ground collapsed above them, they kept running, following the tunnel down, down, down into the dark.

They kept going until they literally ran into Glimfinkle and fell down in a tangle of limbs and paws and squeaks. The gnome shoved them away. He stood up and brushed himself off.

"Blasted rodents!" he said. "Never lookin' where yer goin'."

Twig sat back on his haunches and felt all over himself. He was alive! But . . . fur. He was covered in fur!

"Rats!" he squeaked.

"I think you mean mice," Vile replied. Even in Mouse, she sounded sarcastic. "Now what, Twig?"

"Wait a bloomin' minute ..." said Glimfinkle. "Twig? Is that ye and the hag?"

"Yeah," squeaked Twig. "I think we're mice."

Glimfinkle laughed so hard that he fell over and rolled around on his back.

"It's not funny. I didn't mean to turn us into mice," squeaked Twig. "I only meant to make us smaller."

"That's the problem with wizards," said Glimfinkle

when he'd finally stopped laughing. "Ye never think things through, ye just go poppin' off spells willy-nilly. It's a wonder any of ye survive. Yer lucky I speak Mouse, ye know."

"Where are we?" asked Vile, glancing around. "I can't see anything."

"Some kind of rodent warren, I expect," said the gnome, looking about the place. As gnomes primarily dwelt underground, his vision was pretty good even in bad circumstances. He took a sniff. "Vole, maybe."

"How are we going to get out of here? We can't go back the way we came."

"We'll have to follow it around," said Glimfinkle. "It'll come back out somewhere. There's always a back door. Rodents are sneaky like that. But some light would help, don't ye think, wizard?"

"Right," said Twig. "Illuminate the night and make it bright!" he squeaked.

There was a spark ... then another ... but they both fizzled and died. There was silence for a moment in the pitch

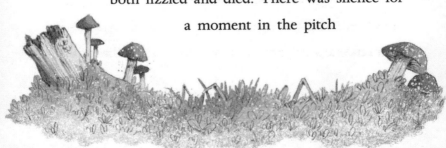

black of the tunnel.

"Er, Twig," said Vile, "please don't tell me you can't do magic now."

Twig tried again, but the same thing happened. So he tried again. The dark seemed to press in around them from all sides. Twig gulped, his heart hammering in his ears. Why did the dark feel so ... *dark*?

"Well, this is a pickle," said Glimfinkle after a moment. "Just how does yer wizard magic usually work anyway?"

"Well ... usually I just think about what I want to happen and then say the spell. Rhyming helps make it more stable," said Twig.

"So, no need for staffs or potions or smelly goop or whatnot, then?"

Twig shook his little mouse head. "Ripplemintz said those things can help provide focus, but ... well, no. Not really. At least, I never needed them before."

Not like he had a lot of experience – he'd only been the world's greatest wizard for less than a week. And now here he was, stuck in mouse form. And he'd turned Vile into one too! Although ... if he was a mouse then he didn't have to worry about showing up for the Euphonium. But that thought didn't really make him feel any better. Having to compete against a bunch of unstable wizards was probably better than being stuck as a mouse.

"Most wizards like to be flash," he heard Vile say. "Style over substance. And most of them aren't as powerful as Twig. He doesn't need that stuff."

Twig had just been wondering whether or not a staff would help, but now he swallowed the thought.

"Have ye ever heard any mouse poetry before?" asked Glimfinkle.

"I didn't know mice wrote poetry," he managed to squeak out in surprise. What in the kingdoms was the gnome talking about?

"Well they do. And, ye see, yer speaking Mouse and all, but yer not really talkin' *like* a mouse. Ye understand?" Glimfinkle cleared his throat. "Lemme give ye an example. This one here's a famous poem by a mouse and ye have to remember that he was considered to be one o' the cleverest of his kind. Birchbark, his name was." Glimfinkle stepped forwards and planted his hands firmly on his hips, chin up.

"Rain wet

Sun warm

Moon dark light

Seeds good."

When he was done, the gnome took a bow.

"I could write a poem better than that," squeaked Vile.

"Exactly!" said Glimfinkle. "Absolute rubbish! And nothin' at all like a glorious gnome poem. Why, *those* are bloomin' epic and can take up to three days to recite! But what I'm tryin' to say is that maybe yer spells are too complicated for a mouse to be castin', even one with your power?"

Twig thought a moment. It *did* make a lot of sense. Maybe the gnome was right?

"Light," he said, concentrating as hard as he could. A new spark appeared, but this one held and grew brighter and brighter until it stopped and hovered above them, like a firefly.

"And there ye go," said Glimfinkle, sounding pleased. "Now we just need to find our way out o' here before whatever lives here comes back." He stomped off and

they followed after him, the little light bobbing above
their heads.

10

IN WHICH WHOOO KNOWS WHAT WILL HAPPEN?

Two hours later, they finally saw their first glimmer of moonlight. Vile, squeaking her excitement, was the first out. Twig followed right behind. The cold night air felt amazingly crisp on Twig's whiskers and he felt more alive than he remembered ever feeling before, but at the same time he felt incredibly exposed. After all, he was tiny. And there were so many noises that he'd never noticed before while in his human body. Now he definitely understood why mice were such twitchy creatures.

"What was that?" squeaked Vile, after something

near them rustled and something else hooted. She was obviously feeling it too.

"I don't know," squeaked Twig.

"Just hurry up and change us back, will you?" squeaked Vile. "I don't like being this small out here in the open."

Twig took a look around. Trees loomed above them, but they were in a relatively large clearing. There was room for them to both become normal-sized again without winding up stuck in the middle of a bush. He thought for a moment. There weren't many things that rhymed with mouse.

"Now that we're secure, if it isn't premature, no longer a mouse nor a louse!" he spelled. A dozen sparks shot high up into the air and the area around them brightened for a moment, dazzling his eyes, but then it faded away.

They were still mice, not a whisker out of place.

"Ye've gone too complex again," said Glimfinkle. "And ye might want to cool it with the fireworks, unless ye want to announce to the whole of the forest exactly where ye are."

"Just make us big!" squeaked Vile.

"No way," squeaked Twig, imagining the worst. "What

120

if we wind up as giant mice?"

Glimfinkle snorted. "Now, that I'd pay good coin to see."

"Shut up," squeaked Vile, "or I'll bite you."

Glimfinkle moved away and put Twig in between himself and Vile.

"I guess I need some time to think up a proper spell." What rhymed with mice? Ice? Entice? Lice? Yuck!

"Well, I don't fancy sittin' around here like lame ducks while yer doin' yer thinkin'," whispered Glimfinkle. "Not after that light show. I don't trust our luck if we stay here long." He whistled a bird call and after a few moments Beaky flew down to land in front of them and cheeped a complaint at them.

"Poor bird's been circling for ages lookin' for us," said Glimfinkle. He gave the magpie a pat and scratched the top of his head.

"Could he carry us all somewhere safe?" asked Twig.

"Three of us? He's no' a bleedin' hawk, so no," said Glimfinkle.

"Hurry up," squeaked Vile. "My hag sense is going wild. We need to get out of here."

Her beady little mouse eyes were darting in every direction.

"OK, OK," squeaked Twig. "Just give me a second."

Did anything rhyme with normal? What if he skipped rhyming completely?

"I mean it, Twig. Something's wrong. I can feel it," squeaked Vile.

He looked over at her and his eyes widened. Her fur was literally standing on end like she'd been hit by lightning. Good thing her hag sense didn't do that when she was her normal human self, though maybe it explained why her hair was always a mess.

"Maybe I could make him strong enough to carry us while we're still mice ... Would that be OK with him?" After his disastrous emergency attempt at making them small (and Vile's understandably angry reaction), Twig was feeling very cautious about spell casting on others without asking first.

"Just do it already!" Vile was running around in circles,

unable to contain herself.

"I have to get it right!" squeaked Twig. She wasn't helping at all. He didn't want to accidentally blow up Beaky.

Vile's nervous circling brought her out of the shadows and into a patch of moonlight. There was a sudden rush of wing-fed air. An owl! It swooped down and snatched her and flew up. Her hag sense had been dead on.

Glimfinkle let out a startled swear. Beaky twittered something. Twig hoped it was a "yes". They needed him now.

"Strong bird," Twig squeaked, keeping the spell simple.

A swirl of sparks surrounded Beaky and he shook himself off as if someone had poured a cup of water over him. Twig scampered over to him. Glimfinkle helped heft him on board.

"Follow that owl!" squeaked Twig. Beaky shot off into the sky.

The owl seemed to realize they were giving chase as it dodged around trees in a crazy zigzag pattern. Beaky was slowed down by carrying them, but the recent infusion of strength seemed to have given him new purpose. He hovered just on the tail of the owl.

Vile was screaming curses and hexes left and right. Twig wasn't sure if they would work in mouse-speak or not, but if they did, that owl and all of his descendants were in big, big trouble.

"Hang on, Vile!" he squeaked as loudly as he could, then "Fast" he be-spelled Beaky. The magpie took off with startling speed.

It was a largish owl, mostly brown, with feathers streaked with white. It was bigger than Beaky, but it definitely wasn't used to being screamed at by its prey, or chased by a super-fast magpie for that matter. Even Glimfinkle was shrieking at it in unintelligible hoots and tweets that Twig could only assume were owl-speak.

"Can ye get me any closer, Beaky?" yelled the gnome.

The magpie put on another burst of speed, his wings a blur against the night sky. It was all Twig could do to hang on, his little mouse paws scrabbling to keep hold of Beaky's harness. He could feel his heart going a million miles a minute. They were just a wings breadth away now, closer, closer . . .

"Give back our hag, ye blasted feather-brained smell-feast!" Glimfinkle pulled a gold coin out from under his hat and chucked it at the owl's head. It PLUNKED off, tumbling down one way while the owl banked the other, hooting angrily.

The owl made a desperate climb upward and then, when Beaky followed, it dropped Vile in mid-swoop, almost like it was aiming for the magpie's head.

For a moment, everything seemed like it was in slow motion and then Vile's hexing turned into pure high-pitched squealing as she hurtled towards the ground far below. Beaky put on the brakes, but tangled himself up as he tried to change direction. Twig reached out a useless paw as Vile tumbled past them. She was going to plummet to her death if he didn't do something, but he didn't know what to do. Things were going too fast. He didn't have time. He needed more time!

"STOP!" he commanded, mustering all of the magic he could feel inside himself. It wasn't so much a spell as it was a word of power, and he didn't even know if it would do anything. But as soon as the word was spoken, everything, absolutely everything . . .

stopped.

Vile hung in the air, still a good drop from the ground. Beaky was frozen, his wings spread wide. Glimfinkle's mouth was open in a shout, but nothing was coming out. The whole of the Eternal Forest and maybe even beyond was silent as even the leaves in the trees were stilled. There was no breeze, not even the barest of whispers of wind.

Twig took a deep breath and then another. His throat hurt a little from the word he'd shouted. He closed his eyes for a moment and thought.

"Feather-light," he whisper-squeaked, picturing in his mind Vile drifting gently to the ground. And then, with as much force as he could muster, "NOW!"

Vile floated gently down, drifting like a feather from side to side. She'd stopped squealing when Twig had made everything stop, but she didn't start up again when he made everything go, so that was a bonus. He hoped she hadn't fainted. Glimfinkle, on the other hand, came out of the spell yelling even louder than before.

"Wot was *that*? What did ye do, ye ruddy bumbling wizard?"

Beaky, released from the spell, fell into a graceful glide and circled down, landing about the same time as Vile. He seemed fairly calm, considering Glimfinkle was still screaming as they landed.

"By St Boogar and all the saints at the backside door of purgatory! That was some bloomin' big magic!" the gnome yelled. "I thought ye couldn't do anything like that while ye were stuck as a mouse!"

"I didn't think I could either," squeaked Twig.

"The things ye *don't* know could fill a blasted book," said Glimfinkle, dismounting Beaky with a grumble. Twig tried to jump down gracefully, but wound up falling off in a heap.

Vile straightened out her dress, now berry-stained, rimmed with mud, and with a number of new holes from the owl's talons. She was shaking. She had, after all, nearly been eaten.

"Where are we?" asked Twig. "Is your hag sense tingling? Is it safe?"

Vile took a deep breath. She sniffed the air, her whiskers twitching. "I don't feel anything," she squeaked.

"If ye can do big magic like that, there's no need for ye to worry about *anything* that's in these woods," said Glimfinkle.

"Big magic?" squeaked Twig. He wasn't sure if "big" was the right word. It wasn't nearly enough to explain how that spell had made him feel: the burning rush when the word had left him, the feeling of something exiting his body and then coming back threefold. And the aching tiredness he felt now, like he could sleep for days.

Glimfinkle snorted and held out an arm, pushing up his sleeve. "Look at that, would ye? The hairs on me arm are standin' right up at attention like me mam was givin' me what for. Big magic, that's what."

"I don't know what else is out there," squeaked Vile, "but I agree with the gnome. That was big magic, Twig. Huge. I think you might have stopped time, at least in the forest. Maybe in all the kingdoms!" She sounded stunned, even in mouse.

Twig sat, curling his tail around him. He didn't know what to say. Had he stopped ALL time? Was that even possible? What would Ripplemintz say if he knew? Time seemed like something that one definitely shouldn't muck about with. But he hadn't had a choice.

Beaky let out a *chirp cheep chirp chirp*. Glimfinkle nodded and the magpie flew up.

"Beaky's goin' to see what's what. But if I were a bettin' gnome, I'd say we're safe for now. Anythin' with half a brain must've felt *that* spell and taken cover."

The magpie circled around above them for a few moments while Vile patted her fur back into place and Glimfinkle wandered around mumbling something about his gold coin. Twig watched them both, his eyes feeling heavy. Beaky landed and chirped at the gnome.

"That owl led us a merry chase. At least Beaky says it was in the right direction. We're closer to the oracle than we were before."

Twig still didn't have any idea what spell he was going to cast to fix them. He knew he had to keep it simple for it to work in mouse-speak, but that was all he knew for certain. That last spell had been big, he knew it himself, had felt the spell burn as it went up his throat and expand as it had left his lips, but he didn't really know *how* he'd done it. He'd panicked.

The more magic he did, the less he felt he knew.

He also knew he *definitely* did not want to be stuck as a mouse for ever, small or otherwise.

"I'm exhausted," he finally squeaked, his voice quivering. "Can we rest? Please?"

Vile stopped her preening to really look at him. "Yeah," she squeaked after a moment, "I'm tired too. Let's go on in the morning."

"But—" began Glimfinkle, but Vile headbutted him and knocked him over. "Oh, all right then. Might as well wait for break of day."

They found a berry bush and crept beneath it. Twig and Vile both curled up into small, round, furry balls, tucking their noses into their fur. Glimfinkle made himself a space underneath one of Beaky's wings and began snoring almost immediately.

Twig had nearly fallen asleep when he felt a nudge against his back. He raised his head to look into Vile's unblinking dark eyes.

"Er, thanks," she squeaked. "For saving my life." Then she rolled over and pulled a leaf over her furry little head.

"You're welcome," squeaked Twig to her back.

11

IN WHICH THERE IS
SOMETHING VILE

Twig awoke with a start, unsure of where he was, or even *who* he was for a moment. The fact that he was still a mouse might have had something to do with it.

Or it might have been the shouting match that Glimfinkle and Vile were having directly over the top of his head.

"I still say ye owe me a gold coin!" yelled the gnome.

"How do you figure that, exactly?" Vile was sitting back on her haunches, a half-eaten berry clutched in her paws. It was hard to read her expression underneath the fur, but Twig could tell from her tone that she wasn't in a very good mood.

"If it weren't fer me usin' one of me hard-earned coins to brain that fool owl with, you'd've been gobbled up fer sure." Glimfinkle had his hands on his hips, his hat slightly askew. He didn't sound very happy either.

"If anyone saved me, it was Twig," squeaked Vile. "Right, Twig?" She poked at him with one of her paws.

"Er ..." Twig scuttled backwards so he wasn't stuck directly between them.

Glimfinkle humphed. "I had me hand in it," he grumped. "Ye owe me a coin. I been lookin' all over these dratted woods and I can't find it anywhere." He pulled a twig out of his beard and threw it away.

"We've got more important things to worry about," squeaked Vile.

"More important than gold?" asked Glimfinkle. "There ain't no such thing."

She threw the remains of the berry at the gnome. It bounced off his nose, leaving behind a purple splotch. "Yes, there is. Changing back. I'm sick of being a mouse." She turned to Twig. "You slept practically for ever. It must be half ten by now and I've had to listen to this dratted gnome complain all morning."

Half ten? Twig felt like he'd barely slept at all. He wiped the sleep out of his eyes.

"Ye could magic me up a gold coin," said Glimfinkle, turning on Twig. "Now that yer finally awake."

"Sorry, I can't," squeaked Twig.

"Duh," squeaked Vile. "Anyone knows that. If wizards could just magic up gold whenever they wanted, why'd any of them ever bother getting a job?"

"Bloomin' useless, wizards and hags both," said Glimfinkle. "That was me lucky coin."

"Sorry," squeaked Twig again. His tummy rumbled. He felt like he hadn't eaten in days.

"Useless?" squeaked Vile. She picked up another berry and bounced it in the palm of her paw. "Say that again, gnome."

"I can't even think with you two going at it!" squeaked Twig. He grabbed the berry from Vile and took a big bite of it. He was so hungry.

"Just change me back and I'll step on him," squeaked Vile.

"That'll solve that problem."

"I'll bite yer big toe!" sputtered Glimfinkle.

"Can't you two be quiet?!" squeaked Twig, standing up on his hind paws. He hadn't meant to, but the last came out as a half-formed spell. Sparks shot out but then fizzled almost immediately.

"Urk," squeaked Twig and fell over flat.

Beaky flew in from overhead and landed between the gnome and the hag. He chirruped something angrily and stepped over to Twig, carefully picking him up with his beak and setting him gently against a rock so he was sitting up.

"Twig, are you OK?" squeaked Vile.

"Any fool can see he's not," said Glimfinkle and was about to say more, but Beaky interrupted with another angry chirp.

"I'm just tired," squeaked Twig. "And hungry. I think that spell took it out of me."

"It didn't even work," said Glimfinkle. "See? I'm not quiet at all."

"Not that spell. The big magic last night," squeaked Vile.

She picked another berry from the bush and handed it to Twig. He stuffed the whole thing in his mouth and chewed.

Beaky twittered at Glimfinkle, cocking his head to the side.

"Beaky says he can carry Twig and let him rest some more on the way to the oracle," said Glimfinkle grudgingly. "And that we should shut it with the arguing. Or else."

Beaky puffed his feathers up and stared Vile right in the eye. She shut her mouth with a snap and held out another berry to Twig. He swallowed the rest of the last one and stuffed this one in his mouth too. Vile fed him more until his belly was rounded and full to the brim.

Glimfinkle and Vile hopped aboard Beaky, then the magpie gently picked up Twig and held him cradled in his claws.

The magpie flew straight and strong like a black-and-white arrow through the sky, his strengthened wings pumping. The morning air was crisp and cool, ruffling their fur. Twig closed his eyes and let the air flow over him.

It was late afternoon when Beaky flew them over Vine Gorge. The large ravine was completely entwined with vines, which made it nearly impassable by foot, unless you were small enough to creep between the clinging vines, but if you were that small it would probably take you *weeks* to cross it. No one knew exactly how deep it went in the centre, because no one could see the bottom.

"Look!" squeaked Vile, "There's one of the two fairy bridges!"

Her cry woke Twig from his nap. He opened his eyes and peeked down. The bridge definitely looked fairy-built. There were no right angles and it almost seemed like it had grown rather than been constructed. It glowed with a greenish-golden light that flickered through the leaves.

"Yeah," said Glimfinkle. "Been there since before my Dah was born and he's near four hundred. Them fairies knew how to build, I'll say that for 'em."

Beaky flew over the top of the bridge, much to Twig's relief – Vine Gorge was beautiful, but it wasn't something he wanted to accidentally fall into. He didn't think he'd ever be able to find his way out again. Twig had heard stories of people who hadn't, and for the very first time he believed them.

After the gorge, they found themselves flying over low foothills that gradually grew taller and taller until the terrain grew rocky and steep. A trail below them squeezed between boulders and along ledges that were sometimes so small that Twig wondered how anyone traversed them.

Beaky chirped. "We're nearly there!" called Glimfinkle, "And about time. Me bum's been asleep for an hour at least."

Twig caught a glimmer of blue up ahead, and before he knew it they were flying over a rocky pool of such a deep blue that it looked like a giant had scooped up a big bucket of the sky and plopped it down. Not a ripple disturbed its surface. Slowly, Beaky took them down, down, until they were nearly skimming the water.

"There's the cave," said Glimfinkle, as they landed in front of the gaping entrance.

"Obviously," said Vile.

There was an old wooden marker propped up against one side of the entrance. It said "The Oracle" in large letters, and underneath that, in smaller ones was written, "Please have your question ready."

Beaky carefully set Twig down on a clump of grass. Vile and Glimfinkle dismounted and stretched.

"Did yer get a good rest?" asked Glimfinkle.

"I do feel better, thanks," squeaked Twig, standing up to stretch himself. The spell he hadn't meant to cast may not have worked, but Beaky's threat had. The gnome and the hag had been quieter on the flight to the cave than they had been on any other point in the trip. Possibly ever.

"Good," squeaked Vile. "Change us back now."

"Yer awfully demanding," said Glimfinkle, "fer such an ungrateful cheapskate hag."

"Shut it about the coin, already," squeaked Vile. "I'll find you a new one later. After I'm human again. Twig? Get on with it."

"Would you two stop already?" Twig squeaked. "Arguing all the time isn't helping anything." He turned his back on them, which would have been much more effective if he hadn't been a small, fuzzy mouse. He was already missing the quiet of the flight, when all he'd heard was the sound of the wind.

"You're one to talk," squeaked Vile. "I don't see you offering up any suggestions or casting any spells, O great and powerful wizard. How about you fix us before something else tries to eat me?"

"Fine," snarled Twig, one more thing that didn't translate well as a mouse. It sounded more like a strangled squeal than anything else, which annoyed him even more. He couldn't even sound properly angry.

"Be Vile," he spelled, twitching his tail about for emphasis. "If that's what you want to be."

Fiery sparks swirled around her tiny mouse form, then expanded as her body did. Glimfinkle and Twig both stumbled back as the swirl grew larger and larger, like he had unleashed a small tornado on her. Twig squeezed his eyes shut, afraid to look now that he'd done it. He hadn't thought about the spell at all, he'd just flung it out there. What had he done? What was going to happen to her?

He felt the spell subside, gone like his anger. The sage had once said that spells cast in anger were strong, but unstable: changeable, even, and therefore not recommended as they weren't generally reproducible. Why did he only remember these things *after* he'd cast a spell?

"Whoo!" whooped Vile. "You did it!"

Twig opened his eyes and craned his neck to look up and up. She seemed OK and Vile-shaped, but it was hard to tell as she was twirling around and around in celebration so fast that he couldn't really see her other than as a swirl of ugly puce fabric and red hair.

He breathed out a sigh of relief. He hadn't done anything bad after all. Everything was back to normal.

Vile danced about some more and then, dizzy, stumbled over to the edge of the Pool of Truth and Wisdom. She fell to her knees and took a good look at herself in the water.

"Oh, Twig," she said, in a small, quiet voice that Twig had never heard from her before.

"Turn around, ye wee hag, and let us see," said Glimfinkle.

Vile turned and for a moment Twig's mouse-born fight-or-flight instinct took over and he wanted to run and hide. Vile looked like she had the first time he had met her, but this time the long, knobbly nose was her own and not a parsnip. Warts had appeared on her face and hands, slightly greenish, and this time they were real and not pieces of pasted-on mushroom. She opened her mouth to say something and Twig recoiled from the rotten, gap-toothed horror of it. She looked a proper hag now. He'd done it this time. He was dead. Deader than dead. She was going to kill him.

"Oh, Twig," she said again, "it's perfect! How did you know?"

The only noise that came out of him was a strangled squeak.

Vile turned back to the water and bent even closer to the reflection of her horribleness. She preened, patting her matted hair with bent and crooked fingers. Her formerly brilliant hair now looked like it had never been washed in her entire life. Even the colour of it had dulled from the fiery sunset red it had been to a burnt umber like the depths of a banked fire. The robe Ripplemintz had given her, already stained and torn from their travels, was the only thing that had remained the same. That, and her brilliant green eyes.

Glimfinkle cleared his throat. "Ye know how I was hopin' ye could magic me a bit taller, Twig? Ferget I asked. I'm good as I am."

"Are you going to make yourself look better too?" asked Vile after she was done admiring herself. "I mean, not that you look bad or anything. Just, you know, if you wanted to look more, um, impressive for the Euphonium or something."

"I wasn't planning on it," Twig managed to squeak out, too surprised to be offended. He'd been sitting there wondering if he should tell her that he hadn't made her ugly and hideous on purpose. He'd pretty much come to the conclusion that it would be in his best interests to keep quiet.

It was definitely time to change himself back, though he really didn't want to wind up like Vile. He squeezed his eyes tight shut and imagined himself as he'd always been. "Twig," he squeaked firmly. "Just Twig."

The spell took hold and spun him this way and that in a swoosh of sparks. He tucked and rolled as it shook him

143

about, trying to hold on in his mind to who he was. He was Twig Thicket, born and raised in Muckwood. Sixth born of twelve. Son of Hedge and Nettle Thicket. Apprentice to Ripplemintz the Sage. Skinny, brown-haired, long-fingered, and with knobbly knees.

Paws became hands, fur shrank away and disappeared, limbs lengthened, knees became knobbly. Twig found himself curled into a ball on the ground when the spell was finished, his eyes still tightly shut. He wiggled his fingers and toes. They felt OK. He reached up and felt his nose. Still slightly pointy. No warts.

"Oh, just open yer eyes already, boy, ye look every bit as silly as ye used to."

Twig did, and sat up, patting himself all over. *Yes*. He was Twig-shaped again. He scuttled over to the pond and took a look. He looked the same too. He considered himself. Maybe Vile had been right. He could have given himself some bigger muscles or made himself a little taller. It wouldn't have hurt.

12

IN WHICH THERE IS A CAVE

"Who's first?" asked Glimfinkle, pointing towards the cave entrance. "I nominate the hag."

"I should go first," said Twig. "It's my question, after all." He wasn't honestly sure why he'd volunteered. Dark, damp places weren't his favourite.

"Whatever," said Vile. "You could fit a dragon in there. It's not like we won't all fit."

"Right," said Twig. "Er, let's go then."

"Have ye got yer questions ready?"

"What?" asked Vile.

Glimfinkle pointed at the sign. "Always follow the

145

rules with things like oracles," he said. "That's what me Dah and Pah always said. Gah too."

"Dah? Pah?"

Glimfinkle looked at Twig like he was a half-wit. "Dah's me dad, Pah's me grandfather, and Gah's me great-granddad. And Grah's—"

"Yeah, yeah, I've got my question. Can we get a move on?" Vile's fingers twitched like she was itching to cast a hex.

Twig held up a hand. "Wait, do we only get one question?"

"That's generally how it works," said Glimfinkle.

Well, there really was just the one question he wanted to ask anyway. That's why he'd come all this way. But what about Vile?

"What are you asking, Vile? Are you going to ask where your aunt is?"

"*Tch*, don't waste an oracle question on somethin' like that," interrupted Glimfinkle. "We're talkin' a once-in-a-lifetime experience, here."

"The gnome's got a point," said Vile.

Glimfinkle was so surprised at her agreement that

his mouth fell open.

"So, what are you going to ask?" asked Twig.

"I'm not saying," said Vile. "It's bad luck."

Twig had never heard that before. Wasn't that for wishes on a falling star and good dreams? Maybe she just didn't want to tell him. Well, fine then.

"Let's go," said Twig, and popped the gnome into a pocket so his little legs wouldn't slow them down.

Vile followed close behind, while Beaky stayed outside. He didn't care for tunnels.

The inside of the cave was dry, but only dimly lit by some phosphorescent lichen and fungi. It put an eerie greenish glow on everything. The path, however, was clear and they followed it deeper and deeper into the cave.

"It's awfully quiet," said Twig finally.

"What did you expect?" asked Vile. "The oracle lives past Vine Gorge along a perilous path that no normal horse could travel along."

"Probably don't want to be bothered," said Glimfinkle, his voice muffled from inside Twig's pocket. "Still, I imagine she knows we're coming, bein' the oracle and all."

They kept going. The tunnel narrowed and then opened up again into a large hollow with stalactites and stalagmites. The path meandered around the lumpy protrusions to another tunnel on the other side. This one was better lit, with glowing crystals complementing the gleaming plants and mushrooms. It was very pretty, if you liked that kind of thing. Twig was thinking he liked the sun better.

"That must be it," said Vile, pointing to a door ahead.

Twig had raised his hand to knock, as it seemed the polite thing to do, when the door swung open. A slight young woman with long, flowing hair that went

almost to her knees stood there. She wore a simple cotton homespun dress of white, though the edge of it had turned brown from dragging through the dirt. She didn't have any shoes on, but she didn't seem to mind. She wiggled her toes in the dirt.

"Hullo," she said.

"Um, hello," said Twig. She stared at him expectantly. "Who are—" he started to say, but Glimfinkle erupted out of his pocket with a yell that would have made a banshee proud. Twig barely managed to catch the gnome before he hit the ground.

"Shut up, ye fool! By all the shrubberies, don't waste yer question on somethin' so bleedin' obvious!" He shook his head at the woman. "Bloomin' rookie mistake, that is, no doubt about it. Or a dirty trick, mebbe."

The woman smiled at the gnome and shrugged her shoulders.

"You're the oracle," said Twig, feeling rather stupid, but making sure not to make it sound like a question. He'd thought oracles were supposed to be old and wise and wrinkly somehow. This one looked about the same age as his sister Minnow.

"Yes," she said. "I've been expecting you. You're right on time." She smiled again and nodded at Vile.

149

"You've all got a question, I think. Perhaps the same one, more or less."

"Am I ever going to be a proper hag?" Vile blurted out without preamble.

Twig turned to her in surprise. That wasn't what he had expected her to ask at all.

The oracle put her hands together, standing primly, except for her toes, which were still wriggling about in the dirt. "One cannot be what one is not. You are what you are what you are," she said solemnly with a nod that seemed very final. "That goes for both of you." She looked back at Twig and winked. "I'll give you that one for free."

Twig had never seen a person deflate before, but that's what it looked like Vile did. Her shoulders slumped, her head dropped. Even her hair wilted. He patted her on the back, but she moved away.

"Any other questions?" the oracle asked brightly, looking from Twig to Glimfinkle, as if she hadn't just crushed all of Vile's hopes and dreams.

"Am I ever going to be as grand as I ought?" asked Glimfinkle as he dangled from Twig's fingertips.

"Oh, yes, I forgot about you, little gnome. You get the same answer," she said, bending down to look him right in the eye. "One cannot be what one is not. You are what you are what you are."

Glimfinkle went slack, looking as small as Twig had ever seen him look, which was pretty small considering he was a gnome.

Twig was a bit afraid to ask a question himself now. Did she give the same answer to everything? That was a bit lazy. He cleared his throat. Perhaps it was best to be direct.

"How can I remove my curse?" he asked. That seemed straightforward enough. She couldn't possibly say the same thing as before, even if she had said that the answer she'd given to Vile and Glimfinkle went for him too. It definitely wasn't the answer to *this* question.

The oracle considered him for a long unblinking moment. "What a stupid question," she finally said. "I'm not even going to dignify that with an answer." She turned about with a flounce and slammed the door right in their faces so fast that Twig didn't even have time to shut his mouth, which had dropped open in surprise. She *definitely* reminded him of his sister Minnow.

"Well, that was a bejabberin' disappointment if there ever was one," said Glimfinkle. "I'd always thought meetin' the oracle would be a bit less depressin' than that."

"She didn't even *try* to answer my question," said Twig. He squared his shoulders. "*I* think she was rubbish. Maybe she isn't even really the oracle. She certainly didn't look like one to me." He patted Vile again. "Don't pay her any mind."

Vile mumbled something that he couldn't hear.

"What?"

"Nothing," she growled. "At least *you're* still the world's most powerful wizard."

The walk out of the cave felt like it took even longer than the walk in, but that might have been because no one said anything. What was there to say? The entire trip to see the oracle had been a complete waste of time. Actually, everything since they had left Muckwood had been completely fruitless. Witch Wormwood had been unable or unwilling to help them, they'd almost been eaten by an ogre, he'd accidentally turned them into mice, Vile had nearly been eaten by an owl, and now the oracle had basically dashed all their hopes.

When they came out into the sunlight, blinking, Glimfinkle stopped and faced Twig. "Wot now?" he asked.

"It's obvious, isn't it?" asked Vile. "We go to the Euphonium."

"I guess," said Twig, forcing himself to answer since Vile and Glimfinkle were both looking at him. He didn't really want to think about any of it. He should never have become Ripplemintz's apprentice. He could be at home right now in the lowly but homey Thicket house being annoyed by the twins. Sure, they were incredibly frustrating, but they didn't pose any actual danger to anything except his patience.

"The king did command it," said Glimfinkle. "So, yeah, we'd best go."

"*You* don't have to," said Vile.

"Wot do ye mean by that?" asked the

gnome, puffing himself up.

"There's no reason for you to come with us now," said Vile, not very sweetly. "You were here to get us to the oracle and what a lot of help *that* was."

Glimfinkle spluttered into his beard. "Well, the king didn't command *you* either. So's there's no reason *you* should go with *us*. Ye can just go on back home and good riddance."

"Um," said Twig. It hadn't occurred to him that there wasn't really any reason for *either* of them to come with him now, but they were both right.

"Home?" said Vile. From the look on her face, she hadn't thought about it either.

"Ye've got yerself a hag hut, haven't ye?"

Twig pictured the hut he'd found her in. No one could call that a *home* by any stretch of the imagination. It was barely upright. "If Agrimony's anywhere," said Twig quickly, "she'll be at the Euphonium. Everyone winds up there, that's what Witch Wormwood said."

Glimfinkle's little face screwed itself up in a few different ways, like he'd eaten a lime and lemon together with a bit of salt on top. "Mebbe," he finally said.

"And even if Agrimony isn't at the Euphonium, Vile's quite, er … useful, don't you think? You, um, both are. Kind of."

Both the gnome and the hag looked at him like he'd grown another head.

"I mean," said Twig, going a bit red, "Vile knows a lot. Like she knew what a Shellycoat was. I'd never even heard of one. And Glimfinkle can speak bird and mouse …"

The hag and the gnome both started arguing at once, pointing fingers at each other.

Twig wanted to scream at them both. He took a deep breath and then another. "It doesn't matter anyway," he said loudly. "Maybe we should all just go home, king or no. I don't see how we can even get there on time." He waved at himself and Vile. "It's not like Beaky can fly us there now that we're human again."

Beaky, who had been watching their exchange from the safety of his perch on top of a boulder, let out a chirruping warble that almost sounded like a laugh.

"Or mebbe he could," said Glimfinkle. "If *I'm* accompanying ye, that is."

13

IN WHICH THERE IS
SOMETHING BIG

"What are you talking about?" asked Twig.

"Beaky says he don't mind if ye want to magic him big enough to carry us all." Glimfinkle rubbed his little hands together. "I think he rather likes what ye did to him already."

"Oh," said Twig.

"That could work," said Vile. "And you've got to at least show up or the king will . . . *you know.*" She drew her finger across her throat.

"Someone there might be able to help me, too," said Twig. After all, it was a gathering of the who's who of witches, wizards, hags and who knows what else.

"I've always wanted to see the Euphonium anyhow," said Glimfinkle. "I been hearin' the stories about it for years. More gold than you can shake a fist at!" He held out a tiny hand. "So's, what do ye think?"

Twig gave him a finger to shake. "Let's give it a try!" He turned to face the magpie. "Are you sure about this, Beaky?"

Beaky bobbed his head up and down.

Twig opened his mouth and then shut it again before saying anything. He had to make sure the spell didn't have any unwanted ... side effects. He stole a glance at Vile. She was scratching at one of her new warts. Yes. He needed to think this one through.

"You're really, really sure, Beaky? You want to be big?"

Beaky squawked loudly and hopped up and down on the boulder.

"He says he's always wanted to be a grand feathered beastie," said Glimfinkle proudly. "That's my Beaky."

Twig took a deep breath.

"Wing and feather

No matter the weather

Let this magpie's dream

Come true with a . . . scream!

A warm wind blew up out of nowhere and swirled around Beaky with a sound almost like a shout, picking up the magpie and twirling him around. As he spun, he grew larger and larger, small feathers flying off of him and larger ones replacing them. His beak stretched in every direction, losing its sleekness. Soon, they couldn't see him for all the feathers swirling around him in a blur of black and white.

"This's takin' a good long while," said Glimfinkle after a moment. "Ye sure ye know what yer doin'?"

Twig *wanted* to say yes but he also didn't want to lie.

Then Beaky let out a loud screech that turned into a full-throated bellow that echoed off the rocks around them. They all took cover as a tornado of feathers exploded out in every direction and a black streak took off into the sky.

"Wot was that!?" said Glimfinkle, crawling out from behind a rock.

"That was totally mad," said Vile, picking herself up off the ground. Her hair was full of feathers.

"Maybe I shouldn't have said 'scream', but I couldn't think of anything else that rhymed with 'dream'," said Twig. He dusted himself off, picking a few feathers out of his own hair. His robes had definitely seen better days.

"Where's Beaky?" asked Glimfinkle, looking around. "Ye didn't blow him up, did ye?"

Another bellow came from above them and a black shape grew larger and larger as it dived towards them. They all watched, open-mouthed, as a bird larger than anything they had ever seen came in for a landing. It didn't look like a magpie at all: it had no white feathers, no gleaming sparkle of mischief in its eyes.

Instead, its feathers were pitch black and its beak had a wicked hook at the end that looked capable of killing pretty much anything it wanted to. Was that really Beaky?

It landed in front of them and turned its head so it

could

give them a

thorough look over with one

of its large round eyes. Twig was pretty sure it was

the same size as the saucers Ripplemintz used for tea.

They had a slightly yellowish colour that was more

than a little disturbing.

"Er ... Beaky?" asked Twig. He wasn't sure if he

should hope this was the magpie or not, but the bird

nodded its head and gave a somewhat familiar chortle

that still managed to sound menacing.

"He ... looks like a boobrie," said Vile.

"A boo— what?" asked Glimfinkle.

"Boobries. They're these huge birds, kind of.

Absolutely vicious and beaks that can pierce a man

straight through." Vile walked a circle around the new

Beaky as she looked him over. "There's usually some

around the swamp. They like water. And eating."

"What do you mean by 'kind of'?" asked Twig.

Vile shrugged and reached out a hand to pat Beaky. "They're shapeshifters. Sometimes they're birds. Sometimes they're bulls. Sometimes they *eat* bulls. You know, things like that. Either way, he's definitely big enough to carry us now."

Twig gulped. "I'm not sure I like the sound of boobries."

"Oh, yeah, I forgot to mention what they sound like. They kind of bellow. Like Beaky just did."

"That's not what I meant," said Twig.

Vile grinned at him. "Just trying to be *useful*," she said. "Besides, it's Beaky. You won't eat us, will you, boy?"

Beaky cocked his head to the side and Twig swore he grinned at them, if that was possible. It didn't make him feel any better. Had Vile said that boobries could eat *cows*?

Beaky bent his head down until he was at Glimfinkle's level. His eye was far bigger than the gnome now. He let out a series of grating chirps and tweets. The gnome stared at him a moment and then gave him a pat on the beak.

"He says thanks," said the gnome.

"You're ... welcome," said Twig. He wasn't sure what else to say.

They set off after Twig spelled them up a new two-person saddle out of some sticks, his battered cloak, and whatever else he could find around. Glimfinkle rode in a little harness attached right next to Beaky's gigantic head so he could give him directions.

Beaky had flown fast before, but now he flew like something was chasing him. Or maybe it was like he was chasing something. Certainly every creature they encountered on land or air fled before him as he passed overhead. Now that they were in the air, Twig could see that the feathers on his wings were tinged red, almost like they were dipped in blood.

They were going so fast that they couldn't really have a conversation, which was just as well. Twig didn't feel like talking. He had no idea what he was going to do when they got to the Euphonium. He had no idea if dragging Vile and Glimfinkle along was a good idea or not. He didn't really think they'd find Agrimony there. Maybe Vile actually would be better off back in Muckwood? Maybe he should have just begged the king for forgiveness? He didn't know anything any more. His thoughts kept going in circles. Should he? Would he? Could he?

He was prodded out of his reverie by Vile's elbow. She leaned back like she had something to say, so Twig leaned forwards so he could hear her over the rush of wind.

"I think we might have a small problem," yelled Vile.

"What now?" asked Twig. The skies ahead were clear. He could even see the treeline not far away. They were finally almost to the plains.

"Are you sure about that spell? I think Beaky's shrinking."

"What?" Twig sat bolt upright and grabbed on to the sides of the saddle. Beaky's wings did a double beat to make up for the disruption. Glimfinkle looked back at them both and shook a tiny fist.

Twig frantically looked around him. The harness and tack had fit Beaky perfectly when they had taken off. Now it was loose and, as he watched, the saddle was slipping sideways a little more with each beat of Beaky's wings.

"We have to land!" he shouted to Glimfinkle. "Tell Beaky we have to land!"

"Wot?" the gnome called back.

"Land!" shouted Twig and Vile together, as the saddle hitched even more to the side.

Beaky was noticeably smaller now and the weight of them plus the saddle was starting to hit him. His wings strained as he struggled to keep them in the air. Twig looked down. The ground seemed really far away. And hard. He had to do something.

Land, by my command!

As if a hand was pressing him towards the earth, Beaky began to glide downwards. He continued to shrink until Twig found himself clutching Vile and trying to make himself as small as possible. He and the hag were both holding on as tight as they could with their knees and it felt like that was all that was keeping the saddle on Beaky.

Glimfinkle had finally noticed and was yelling something, but it was lost in the wind. Beaky's feet dragged through the tops of the trees that marked the end of the Eternal Forest. Down he went, now only barely bigger than a swan. Vile shrieked as the saddle fell off with them on it and they plummeted the remaining few feet to the ground and landed with a THUMP and an OOF. Beaky crashed just ahead of them and they all skidded together into a muddled heap of feathers and boots and broken bits of saddle.

"Ow," said Glimfinkle.

14

IN WHICH TWIG STEPS
ON A THORN

They had crash-landed near a copse of stunted trees. There were no broken bones, though they all had their share of scratches and scrapes. Vile healed them up as well as she could using some yarrow she found growing nearby while Glimfinkle yelled at Twig the entire time.

"I'm sorry!" Twig finally yelled back. "I'm a rubbish wizard and I'm sorry! OK? What else do you want me to say?"

Beaky chirped and hopped on to his shoulder and rubbed his head against Twig's cheek.

Glimfinkle *humphed*. "He says it's not your

fault. Says he ran out of energy and he's got to eat somethin'."

"Me too," said Vile. She pointed up at the darkening sky. "It's time for supper and none of us have had a proper meal in I don't know how long. Should we try the village up ahead? I saw it as we were plummeting towards our doom."

"That'll be Craven," said Glimfinkle. "We made it to the plains, at least."

They dusted themselves off and went into town, Glimfinkle hiding in Vile's pocket. Twig pulled his hood up over his head. He'd been too tired and hungry to even think about magicking up new clothes for them.

It was a small village with just one inn, the Boot and Beetle. They squeezed inside and found it packed full of people. Most were locals, but many were travellers on their way to the Euphonium. The villagers were abuzz with news of the festival and how the tents had magically popped up in the plains of Aramore overnight.

"Didja see Kudzu of the Spire when he came

through?" asked a farmer to no one in particular.

The innkeeper's wife stopped what she was doing to let out a loud, appreciative sigh. "I surely did," she said. "Saw him on that pure white stallion of his, in that fine green silk cloak – what I wouldn't give for that!"

"What I wouldn't give to just have a little chat with him," said an old woman in the corner, lifting up a flagon of ale in toast. "Handsome devil, weren't he?"

"Er," said Twig to the innkeeper, a frazzled man behind the counter, "could I maybe get some bread and—"

"Had good coin too," said the innkeep, ignoring Twig. "Paid me three crowns to pack up a lunch for him and those trained heather pixies he had flying along with him. Titchy little sugar cakes he wanted. Whoever heard of such a thing!"

"Yo!" said Vile, elbowing Twig out of the way. "Some service here or my wiz—"

"Shhh!" Twig hushed her. He pulled his hood closer about his face. "There's no rooms anyway. I'll get some food and meet you back at the clearing."

"But—"

"It's *OK*," said Twig. "Just go." Vile shrugged and elbowed her way out of the inn. It wasn't hard for her. One look and people whispered "hag!" and got out of the way.

Twig finally managed to buy some meat and bread by holding aloft his money pouch and jingling it in the innkeeper's face. He fought his way out of the inn through the buzzing crowd and into the dirt street. It was full dark now, the only light spilling from the windows of the nearby houses.

He saw a purple and green Pixie Post box across the way lit up with fairy lights and decided to send an update to Ripplemintz. It wasn't the news he'd hoped to send, but it was probably best to keep his mentor updated. If the sage even remembered he was gone. Somehow, Twig imagined the old wizard lost in an experiment in his tower and calling for him to sweep up broken glass and then getting annoyed when he didn't show up. The windows had probably already been blown out again.

He knocked with one finger on the tiny door of the pixie house perched on top of an old tree stump. It was made from a large hollowed-out pumpkin with a roof of pinecone shingles and moss. A sort-of tunnel carved from a piece of oak was attached to the side, with a bit of a landing strip.

A pixie popped its head out the door and yawned in Twig's face. "Whaddya want?"

"I need to send a message to Ripplemintz the Sage of Muckwood." Twig fumbled in his sack and pulled out the bag of sugar cubes.

The pixie yawned again. "That's quite a ways, and I'm tired. Can't it wait until tomorrow?"

Twig jiggled the bag. "Two cubes?"

The pixie eyed him. "Three and it's a deal."

Twig nodded and pulled out the cubes. He knew it was too much but it was only sugar and he didn't feel like arguing. He set them down carefully outside the little door.

"So, what's your message?"

"Um . . . I guess . . . no luck with the oracle, so we're off to the Euphonium tomorrow."

The pixie looked him up and down. "To compete?"

"Maybe," said Twig uncomfortably.

"Hmmmm," said the pixie. "Might have to watch that myself." He squinted an eye at Twig. "You don't look like you've a clue what you're about, but there's something about you . . ."

"Er . . . thanks?"

"Well, I'll get your message there. So, go on, get your rest. You're going to need it." The pixie pushed the sugar cubes back inside the house and, a moment later, went shooting out the tunnel and into the sky. "Good luck!" he called down as he disappeared with a POP!

Twig watched the sky for a moment and then walked towards the edge of the village. He hadn't gone far when he stumbled over something sharp.

"Ow!" he said, picking himself up. What had he fallen over in the middle of the street? It was a rosebush, practically dripping with huge flowers. He pulled a thorn out of his thumb and sucked at it. What idiot had planted a rosebush in the middle of the street? Actually . . . it wasn't just roses. The street was carpeted with flowers and herbs: green vines and lilies and forget-me-nots and violets and so much more.

"Ain't it lovely?" said a woman passing by. "Kudzu left that behind him. Everywhere he stepped, there's something left to remind us of him!" She took a big sniff of a rose and danced off down the street.

Twig managed to slink back to meet Vile without talking to anyone else. He shared out the food with everyone and they were so hungry that no one complained about the plainness of the meal. The inn had been nearly sold out. Vile dug right in, like she hadn't eaten in weeks, chewing with her mouth wide open, made all the more disgusting because of how rotted her teeth were now. Glimfinkle turned his back on them all and stuffed himself with cheese so fast that he got the hiccups. Beaky had already flown off somewhere to find himself something to eat.

Twig had to admit that as a group they did not look remotely impressive. At all. What was he doing? He certainly wasn't going to arrive at the Euphonium in style like Kudzu. He was accompanied by a hag in hand-me-down robes, a grumpy gnome with no manners, and a magpie with greater than average strength. He brushed the crumbs off his clothes after eating, noting that they hadn't fared well in their travels. At least he could do something about that.

He took out some thread and shells and the very dead, very flat mouse from the very bottom of Ripplemintz's bag.

"Come here, Glimfinkle," he said, thinking that he'd start with the gnome for practice, just in case.

"Why?" asked the gnome suspiciously. He was cleaning his teeth with a tiny knife.

"I'm going to fix you up."

"No thank ye," said Glimfinkle firmly, nodding his head at Vile, who was picking at one of the warts on her nose while she stared off into the distance in the general direction of the open plains.

"Just your clothes," said Twig.

The gnome stared at him a moment and then finally agreed. Twig fashioned him a new mouse-hide jacket and freshened up the rest of his clothes, making them fit better over the gnome's rounded belly. Glimfinkle patted himself down and gave a grudging thank you.

"Vile?" he asked. "How about you?" Maybe she'd let him remove some warts or at least fix her robes.

"Don't bother," she said. "I'm a hag, aren't I? Don't I look like one now?"

"I guess so," he said, then wished he hadn't. "I mean, yes, of course you are."

Twig took one of the shellycoat's shells, the thread and a bit of cloud and wind to fashion himself a new robe and a cape the colour of the sky. He strode back and forth making sure it floated behind him. That was the bit from the cloud. He thought it looked rather nice.

"What're you bothering sprucing up for anyway? I thought you didn't even want to compete in the Euphonium."

"I don't!" he said automatically. He didn't, did he? "That doesn't mean I can't put my best foot forwards."

Vile sniffed. "Seems to me you'd be better off going in looking like a beggar."

"But if I can't find anyone to help me, I still have to compete," said Twig, not sure if he was trying to convince himself or her.

"Still. If you don't go in all fancy, they'll underestimate you for sure. And then – *Pow!*" She smacked a fist into her hand. "Haven't you ever heard of the element of surprise?"

"The hag has a point," said Glimfinkle. Twig was starting to wonder if the gnome was trying to get on Vile's good side now that she looked a proper hag. He seemed to be agreeing with her more lately. But did she even have a good side?

Twig looked at his new and improved cloak. It was drifting after him, looking slightly grey and cloudy like it was about to rain. The real sky above him was in dark shades of purple streaked with orange. "Well," he said, a bit annoyed, "I've already done it, so that's that. We should get some sleep."

"I'm not tired," said Vile, adding a log to the fire.

"Suit yourself," said Twig. He cleared his throat, stood straight, and waved his hands about like he'd often seen Rimplemintz do in front of company.

"Sticks and leaves,

Protect us from thieves,

Branches come together,

Protect us from the weather!"

The trees around them twisted and bent into the shape of a tiny house, complete with beds of leaves. Twig went in straightaway, not waiting for the others. He didn't care what they did. *He* was going to get a good night's sleep for once. He wasn't going to show up at the Euphonium looking like something the cat had dragged in.

15

IN WHICH THERE ARE NO CURSES

Twig woke up the next morning with a small branch stuck in his back. He hadn't slept particularly well. Instead, he'd lain awake for ages thinking about the Euphonium and what awaited him there. Maybe Vile was right and he should try sneaking quietly in. It didn't feel right, though. He didn't want to hide. He just didn't want to be hounded. Or die. Or get turned into something horrible.

Things like that weren't unheard of at the Euphonium. The wizarding duels were famous for being quite intense. Dangerous enough that they'd even heard about them in Muckwood, like the year the winner had turned his opponent into a toad and then thrown him into the air and exploded him in a shower of toad guts above the crowd. Badger had made up a game called toad ball after that, but it had luckily been short-lived. The toads had wised up quickly.

"Ready?" asked Vile. She'd woken up before him again. He was starting to wonder if she slept at all. Glimfinkle was still snoring.

"Yes," said Twig shortly. He brushed off the leaves and grabbed his cloak. He'd hung it up on a branch the night before where it had drifted above him all night long. Today it was a brilliant blue, tinged with golden yellows along the edges. It looked very cheerful and hopeful. He put it on anyway.

They were on the edge of the Aramore plains and a wide expanse of grasslands stretched ahead of them. Twig fancied he could see the colourful tents of the Euphonium in the distance, but that was probably his imagination. According to the villagers in Craven, they were still a few hours walk away. They would make it by lunchtime if they didn't dawdle.

Vile joined him. She hadn't bothered waking Glimfinkle up but had instead picked up the snoring gnome and stuck him in one of her pockets. At least, that was what Twig guessed based on the noise. They set off, Beaky riding on top of Twig's head. The magpie seemed to be back to normal and none the worse for wear. They followed the carpet of vines and flowers left behind by Kudzu.

"Bit of a show-off, you think?" asked Vile. "I mean, it's pretty, if you like that kind of thing, but it seems a waste. Why not make a proper road, if you're going to go to all the trouble of magicking something up?"

"Maybe he just wants to make the world a prettier place," said Twig. It did look really nice, as it stretched out in front of them, a riot of colours. But it definitely wasn't practical. He'd caught himself on a couple more thorns along the way.

Glimfinkle poked his head out of Vile's pocket. "He even wins nice and pretty," said the gnome with a yawn.

"What do you mean?" asked Twig.

"Don't ye know anything?

The last time Kudzu won the Euphonium, he got the best of Stix of Loudwater by practically drowning him in flowers. Turns out, Stix suffers from wicked hay fever."

"That doesn't sound too bad," said Twig. Definitely better than being exploded.

"Sumac won once," said Vile. "I remember my sister talking about it."

"And . . .?" Twig wasn't sure he wanted to know.

"It wasn't pretty *or* nice," said Vile. "Are you sure you want to know?"

Twig gulped. "Just . . . just tell me, did they make it out alive?"

"Well, if you count living out the rest of your days as an ooze, yeah, sure."

Glimfinkle fell about laughing so hard that he almost tumbled out of Vile's pocket.

Twig glared at the both of them, perhaps a little harder than he meant to. He wished he hadn't asked Vile. He wished they weren't talking about this at all.

Twig stomped on ahead and that was when he realized that he hadn't been imagining things earlier.

The plains of Aramore were so flat that he *could* make out the riot of colour that was the Euphonium. They were that close to his impending doom. Soon, he could even make out individual tents. Red ones, green ones, multicoloured ones, some with stripes, some with dots, some painted in intricate patterns. They met up with other people, drawn to Kudzu's flowery path. There were even some dwarves riding on sturdy ponies, come down from the mountains.

Most of them took one look at Vile and rode or walked on by without a word, except for a stout witch leading a donkey loaded down with every kind of herb you could think of. She was having a grand time picking verbena and yarrow and other flowering herbs in Kudzu's road when she bumped into Vile.

"Excuse you," said the witch.

"Me?" said Vile. "Excuse you!"

The witch shoved Vile out of her way with a hip. "Respect your elders, little hag," she said. She passed them by with a nasty laugh.

Vile thrust her warty fingers at the witch's back, twisting them into an odd shape, and muttered

something that sounded vicious.

Nothing happened.

Vile stopped walking and then pointed at the witch again. Twig recognized what she said this time. It was the same thing she had cast at Sumac when she'd given him boils, but the witch didn't even twitch.

Twig caught up to her. "Vile?"

"My hex didn't work," she said.

"What?" Twig pulled them further away from the trail of flowers and looked at her. She was staring at her fingers like she'd never seen them before.

"It didn't work. She should have popped out all over with huge, festering boils." She looked up from her fingers and met Twig's eyes. "Nothing happened."

"Maybe witches are curse-resistant?"

"Not at all," said Glimfinkle from Vile's pocket. "Maybe the wee hag has bad aim."

Vile pointed a dirty-nailed finger at the gnome and uttered a hex Twig had never heard before. Glimfinkle flinched and ducked down, but nothing happened.

"Don't ye do that!" he said, popping back up. "Ye

gave me a fright, ye hag! Tha's no nice, ye know."

Vile turned to Twig. "My hagging's gone," she said.

"Maybe yer just tired," said Glimfinkle, "though lucky fer me." He patted himself all over like he was checking for boils.

"Maybe," said Vile. She wiggled her fingers and Twig was afraid she was going to try out a curse on him. "It has been a rough couple of days."

They walked on, passing a few groups of farmers and peasants. Twig heard Vile muttering under her breath as they walked by but didn't see anyone break out in boils or sprout extra hair from their nose or anything else disgusting. She grew quiet as they approached the banners and flags that marked the entrance to the Euphonium.

It was easy to see what had stopped her. The Euphonium was huge. They couldn't see the end of it in any direction now that they were close.

"Maybe your Great Aunt Agrimony will be here," said Twig hopefully.

Vile grunted. He didn't say anything else.

There was a tall barrel chested-man standing

guard at the entrance and greeting everyone as they arrived at the main gate, mostly waving people through. He was wearing a long flowing robe of golden silk. He called them to a halt as they approached.

"Spectators or competitors?" the man asked.

"Does it matter?" asked Vile.

The man bent down to peer at her. "Hag," he said with a knowing look. He made a mark on the roll of paper he was holding. Then he turned to Twig, taking in his floating cape and the magpie on his head. "And you?"

"Twig Thicket, wizard of the Kingdom of Muckwood," said Twig, a little louder and more grandly than he'd intended. A few people nearby turned to look in his direction. "I'm here to compete."

"Muckwood?" said the man. "Seriously?" He scratched his head. "Isn't that down by the Midden? Didn't even know there *were* any wizards down that way. I don't know if we've ever had a competitor from Muckwood before."

There was a murmur from the small

crowd around the gate and from the people in the queue behind them. Twig stood up taller, wishing he'd thought to magically clean his boots too. At least he had his cape.

"Well, there's one now," said Vile. "So, are you letting us in or what?"

"By all means," the man said, waving them in to the Euphonium grounds with a bemused look on his face. He pointed to their left. "The registration tent is that way. You can't miss it. Wizard duelling pitch is in the middle, the hag scrap is at the far end, for everyone's safety. Food tents over to the right."

They went through and were immediately swallowed up by the crowd. Twig looked around and took a deep breath as they were jostled this way and that. He wasn't even sure where to look first. Everything seemed to draw his eye at once. There were tents and stalls everywhere, selling everything under the sun.

They'd made it. He couldn't believe they'd actually made it. He wanted to tell someone, wanted to shout it to the world, but everyone he knew was either here with him or all the way back in Muckwood.

"What now?" asked Vile.

"Registration, I guess," said Twig. "Seeing as how I'm already late."

"Me and Beaky have some business to attend to," said Glimfinkle, climbing out of Vile's pocket. Twig gave him a hand up to Beaky.

"What kind of business?"

"None of yer beeswax," said the gnome. "We'll find ye later. Beaky knows how to find ye by now." He took off without another word.

Vile had been pulled in by a stall selling all manner of potion ingredients, from chicken eyes to ground dragon's teeth. Next to it was a stall with love potions, some slightly smoking. On the other side was a witch peddling good-luck charms. Twig was tempted to buy one as you could never have enough luck, but she had no teeth, which didn't seem very auspicious to him considering she was festooned in her own charms.

He had never seen so many people in his entire life. Tall men with red hair and blue tattooed skin, ethereally pale women hiding under floppy brimmed hats that he suspected might be elves, stocky dwarves from the Mountains of Morning, star-struck peasants clutching money purses. It felt like everyone in all of the kingdoms was at the Euphonium.

"You buying or not, hag?" asked the witch running the potion stall.

"Maybe later," said Vile.

"Then move it along, you're blocking the paying customers."

Vile humphed but backed off without flinging even the tiniest curse at the witch. She grabbed Twig's hand and stomped off in the direction of the registration tent. "Come on, let's find the registration tent. You already said you were competing, Mr World's Greatest Wizard."

Twig trailed after her as she stalked through the crowd. Whatever look was on her face was enough to clear a path right quick. But was it his imagination, or were her warts disappearing? She didn't look nearly so bumpy and lumpy as she had earlier. Hopefully his spell was wearing off, though he wasn't sure if she'd be happy about that or not. She still looked plenty ugly, though. Ugly enough to clear their way through the crowd, anyway.

16

IN WHICH THERE IS
SOMETHING NASTY

The registration tent was easy enough to find, just as
the man at the entrance had said it would be. It was
big and red and festooned with banners and flags from
all the kingdoms (except, perhaps, Muckwood, though
Twig wasn't even sure what Muckwood's looked like).
Floating above the tent, in slowly rotating sparking
fiery letters, were the words "Information & First
Aid!" and "Wizards, Witches & Hags Wanted"
and, above all of that, "100th Anniversary of The
Euphonium" was written largest of all, in flashing
letters that looked and sounded a lot like lightning.

As Vile and Twig approached, an unfortunate bird flew near the words and was zapped. It bounced off the roof of the tent and fell off on to the ground, momentarily stunned.

Twig and Vile joined the ragtag queue of Euphonium attendees already there waiting. The queue was long but surprisingly orderly. They could even make out the long wooden trestle table set up in the centre of the tent. Behind it stood a frazzled-looking wizard wearing a grand silver robe covered in stitched symbols of power, a very tall witch who towered over him, and an extremely ugly young hag with the longest, pointiest, twistiest nose that Twig had ever seen.

Vile took one look at the table and promptly turned around to leave, but a few other people had already come in behind them, including one immense wizard that took up the space of three and was also holding a three-legged chicken by the neck with a very annoyed look on his face. Vile bounced off of his chest and into Twig, knocking them both over. There was a bit of a domino effect and soon there was a pile of wizards, witches, peasants, and hags, with Twig and Vile in the middle. It was not a comfortable place to be.

Twig felt the tingle of a spell being cast somewhere off to his right, though he couldn't hear it from his vantage point underneath everyone. He felt himself swept up along with everyone else and put right side up but backwards, which was at least better off than the large wizard, who had been deposited sideways and was flailing about like a beached whale, though he still had a good grip on his chicken.

"Vile!" someone yelled. Twig couldn't tell if it was a good yell or a bad yell, but it was definitely a very loud yell as he heard it clearly over the noise of the disgruntled and confused crowd surrounding him.

He spun around looking for Vile, but in all the mess they had become separated. All Twig could see were elbows and armpits – none of which were Vile's, especially not the elbows of the old hag next to him, who was particularly warty. He pushed his way towards where the voice had come from, but everyone was bigger and taller than he was. He heard a loud, "*Oooof,*" that sounded an awful lot like Vile and some high-pitched shrieking that didn't. What if she was in trouble? She couldn't even protect herself with a curse if she wanted to right now. He had to find her. He waved a hand in the air and cast a spell.

"Don't lallygag,
Show me the hag!"

With a whoosh and a pop, he flew up and over the heads of the crowd, high enough to bang his head on the top of the tent. Then the spell spun him around, robes flapping, and he saw her. The ugly young hag from behind the table had Vile in a chokehold and was knuckling the top of her head with barely concealed glee. No one else seemed to have noticed that she was in trouble as everyone else in the tent was staring up at him, including the hag who had Vile. Her mouth was open, revealing crooked teeth and a bit of half-chewed broccoli that looked like it had been there a very long time. If it wasn't broccoli, he didn't even want to know what it was.

"Let her go!" Twig shouted as he floated in the air, pointing at the hag and trying to ignore all the stares. He hadn't actually intended to be quite so showy but his magic often seemed to have ideas of its own.

The hag grinned a particularly foul grin at him.

"Oh? And who's gonna make me?"

She pulled Vile so close to her that Twig wondered if Vile could even breathe. Her arms were certainly flailing about so fast that she looked like a nest of angry snakes, which probably wasn't far off from her mood.

Twig was working out a good rhyme for "let her go, you slimy hag," when Vile took things into her own hands, or rather, feet. She stomped her boot down upon her captor's foot with all her might and managed to pull her head out of the headlock as the hag gasped in pain and surprise.

Twig waved his hands and swam awkwardly through the air over to Vile. He landed between the two hags, ready for anything. At least having had so many brothers and sisters had prepared him for that. The hag who had attacked Vile straightened up, her nose nearly poking him in the eye. She was even uglier close up, like a hag's version of the ultimate hag.

Amazingly, she was still grinning, now that the initial pain had worn off. "So, found yourself a feisty little wizard boyfriend, then, sister? He looks a little scrawny, but I've seen worse."

This hag was Vile's sister? Twig quickly let go of the follow-up spell he'd been about to cast, letting it dissipate into nothing with a small poof. *"You're* Nasty?" he asked in surprise. She didn't look anything like Vile. At least, not how Vile normally looked before he'd accidentally hagified her. Right now they actually looked pretty similar.

"Shut up," said Vile.

Twig wasn't sure who she was talking to.

"I most certainly am Vile's sister," said the hag, standing tall. "And that's my name, too." She shoved Twig out of the way, and pulled Vile to her, one hand on each shoulder. "And just *what* is my little sister doing here at the Euphonium? And *alive*? I got a rat from Hag Ragwort, who heard from Pleurisy the Unpleasant, who got it first hand from Toadflax, that Great Aunt Agrimony was eaten by a family of ogres while out collecting troll dung in the Midden. I figured you'd've been turned into ogre poo by now."

"So *that's* what happened to her," said

Vile, seemingly unaffected by the news of her great aunt's terrible demise. "I imagine she gave them a horrid tummy ache. But, as you can see, I'm very much alive so you can let me go now." She tried to shrug off Nasty's hands, but her sister wasn't budging.

"Er . . . I'm sorry about your great aunt," said Twig.

"It happens," said Nasty lightly. "After all, we're hags."

"Yeah," added Vile, still wiggling. "It's how she would've wanted to go."

Twig wasn't sure what to say about that, so he said nothing.

"And what," continued Nasty, after taking a good, long look at Vile, "have you done to yourself? Those warts are real!" She finally let go of Vile's shoulders and pried her mouth open. "And your teeth! That's not boot black! They're really rotted!" She released her as Vile tried to bite one of her fingers. "Did someone curse you?" she asked suspiciously.

"No," said Vile.

Twig continued to not say anything. He hoped Vile wouldn't tell Nasty it was his fault. Though, looking at Vile, he thought to himself that she definitely didn't look quite as bad as she had when the spell had first hit her. Her hair was almost back to its normal brilliant colour and the only brown bits left were from dirt. Though there *was* quite a bit of that. And leaves and feathers. She obviously hadn't bothered brushing herself off after sleeping. But the spell was definitely wearing off, maybe because he hadn't intended it to happen anyway. He wondered if the mouse spell would have worn off as well if they had just waited.

Nasty took another long look at Vile and then squashed her up in a huge hug. "Nan would be so proud," said Nasty. "You always were a natural with hexes and now look at you!" She wiped a tear away from her eye. "We're entering you in the hag scrap! Show 'em what the Hornwort's are made of! Oh, I wish Nan were still alive!"

"*I'm* not here to compete" said Vile, shoving Nasty away. "We're here to enter Twig." She pointed at him. "He's a wizard."

Nasty didn't even look in his direction. "Of course you're entering," she said. "You're finally a Hornwort.

You have to."

"Um," said Twig, before he could stop himself. "She was a Hornwort before, too, you know."

Nasty waved a dismissive hand at him. "Whatever. Did you *see* her before?"

"Yes," said Twig. "And she looked fine." He much preferred her that way, though he didn't say that out loud. It wasn't because she was prettier before, but because she'd just been herself. Right now she looked a great deal more like Nasty than Vile. Almost like a paler, shorter copy of her sister.

"But now she looks a *proper* hag," said Nasty. "Like me!"

"She was a proper hag *before!*" insisted Twig. He looked at Vile. Why wasn't she saying anything? He'd never known her to back down from a fight.

"Both of you, shut it!" said Vile finally. "I'm not entering, and you can't make me!" She grabbed Twig's hand and pushed her way over to the showy wizard, shoving people out of the way as she did.

"Twig Thicket. Wizard.

Muckwood," she shouted, as she jabbed a finger at the wizard, almost like she was cursing him. He cringed but Vile glared at him until he wrote it down, looking terrified.

"You're just in time," he squeaked out. "The last elimination round is tonight, but as you're the only entrant from Muckwood, you'll go right through to the next round. Roster will be posted by morning."

"Thank you," said Twig. He wanted to ask a few more questions, like what the elimination round was and where he was supposed to go, but Vile swirled around, a few leaves flying off her head, and pulled Twig out of the tent after her without even another glance at her sister or the wizard.

"I'm putting your name down anyway!" yelled Nasty after them. "I'll see you in the scrap, sister! And don't think I'll go easy on you!"

She was definitely an older sister. Twig could tell.

17

IN WHICH WITCH WORMWOOD IS

"So, *what* is a hag scrap exactly?" asked Twig to Vile's back as she pulled him through the crowd at a fast clip. He was a hundred per cent certain she had no destination in mind as she randomly weaved her way through the crowd.

"It doesn't matter, I'm not doing it," said Vile crossly.

"I didn't say you were," he said. "I just wanted to know what it was. Is it like duelling for wizards?"

Vile slowed down a little, but kept hold of his hand. He felt a bit sweaty and hoped she hadn't noticed. "No. Hags don't stand for all that protocol and the bowing to each other beforehand and all those niceties. Basically, they throw us all into one big arena and we go at it. Last hag standing is the winner."

"Oh," said Twig. "That sounds dangerous."

"Very. Even the local ones can go on for ages. The record was a match held in Dunmire that went on for two weeks. They were finding toads for ages."

"Have you competed in one before?"

"No. They never let me." Vile's grip on his hand increased, as did her speed through the crowd. Maybe he should change the subject.

"So, um, that was your sister, then," said Twig.

"Obviously."

"She's not really very nice," he said, as he bounced off a farmer carrying a burlap sack full of something very squirmy.

"She's a hag," said Vile simply, as if that explained everything. Perhaps it did.

"So are you," he said, before he thought better of it.

She laughed. A very short, sharp laugh with lots of edges to it. "Am I?"

"Yes, you are," he said. "But you're nice . . . er. *Nicer.*" He cleared his throat. "Much nicer."

Vile stopped and spun around so fast he nearly ran into her. "You think I'm nice?"

"Well, yes. Nice-*ish*," said Twig uncomfortably. "And you *are* a proper good hag. Just look at that hex you got off on Sumac. That was brilliant."

Vile looked almost pleased but then she scowled.

"Don't worry. It'll come back," Twig said. "Maybe you're just having an off day or two, right? It happens."

"What will come back?" she said and suddenly she seemed to be looming over him, even though she wasn't that much taller than he was.

"Your hagging," he said in a whisper, wishing that he hadn't started this conversation at all and had just let himself be dragged through the crowd quietly.

Vile dropped his hand like it was a snake that had bit her, and Twig watched as her fingers twitched like she wanted to hex him. She stared at him for a long, long moment and then turned away.

"I—I'm hungry," she said over her shoulder. "I'm getting some food. I'll meet you at the arena at dusk when they post the roster."

"Er, OK," he answered, but she was already swallowed up by the crowd. Twig stood there for a moment, being jostled by everyone coming and going. It was a sea of people, and for the first time it occurred to him that he was a very long way from Muckwood. And alone. *Completely* alone in a strange place without even a gnome to give him bad advice.

Twig looked around but nothing was familiar and he hadn't been paying attention to which way Vile had been leading him. The nearest stall held a collection of shrunken heads. The next one was full of jars, none of which you wanted to look at for too long. He took a few steps in one direction and stopped, then took a few steps back, with no idea where he wanted to go or even where he *should* go.

"You want something, lad?" said the witch at the stall with all the containers. He held out a jar full of newt eyeballs to him. They looked very squidgy.

"Er, no, thanks," Twig said. He tried not to stare. He'd never seen a male witch before, though he'd heard they existed. Ripplemintz said they were as rare as hen's teeth, which their cupboard was always in short supply of.

"Well, move along then," the witch said, losing his smile and the polite tone of voice.

"Please," Twig said, "where is ..." but his voice trailed off. He really had no idea where to go.

The witch glared at him. "Looking for the Witch Fayre?" He pointed to the left. "That way. Go on, then, go gawk." He shook his head to himself. "Peasants," he grumbled. "Don't know a good newt eye from their own hind end."

Twig went the way the witch had pointed, even though he didn't know what the Witch Fayre was. He just knew it was in the opposite direction from where Vile had gone, but she obviously wanted to be alone. Well, fine. He wanted to be alone too, and have a nice wander around the Euphonium without a loud-mouthed gnome or an argumentative hag to distract him.

At first, he thought the Witch Fayre was just another shopping area, until he saw the prize ribbons. As Ripplemintz had once told him, where wizards duelled and hags scrapped, witches made things. Their contribution to the Euphonium seemed to be more about awarding prizes to the best of the best or the worst of the worst. The Witch Fayre showcased both, from the most well-groomed familiar to the strongest love potion to the healthiest deadly nightshade plant.

He wandered from table to table admiring the different entries, stopping a few times in front of particularly interesting submissions – like the largest known collection of dragon scales – and wished he had someone to show them to. He was sure Vile would have appreciated the nightshade in particular and Glimfinkle would have tried to steal a dragon scale to make himself armour out of. But none of the other people walking around looked interested in talking to Twig, so he didn't say anything.

Which meant it was dreadfully boring.

"Ah, Twig, wasn't it?" said a voice from behind, and someone tapped him on the shoulder.

It was Witch Wormwood. She had a blue ribbon pinned to her dress, which was purple and had just as many pockets as the last one he'd seen her in. Maybe even more.

"I see you've made it in one piece to the Euphonium. Well done, you. Always a challenge when operating under a curse, especially at such a young age."

"Um, thanks," said Twig, a little confused. Even though he still wanted to rid himself of the accidental spell, he wasn't sure why she'd think being the world's strongest wizard would have made it harder on him. Everyone else couldn't seem to understand why he wanted to be shut of it.

Witch Wormwood peered at him. "But perhaps

you've managed to lift your curse?" She grinned, winked and elbowed Twig in the side all at once. "So, did you wind up kissing that pretty hag? Was she the one?"

"Excuse me?"

"I saw the way she was glaring at you – if that's not true love, I don't know what is." She sighed dramatically, one hand to her heart. "And there's nothing quite like true love's first kiss." Witch Wormwood sighed again, then straightened up and smiled at Twig. "Well, when you can find it, that is. There's a lot of frogs out there, let me tell you, boy. *A lot* of frogs."

"I'm not ... I mean, I don't ... *what?*" Twig's face was all the various shades of red and he had started sweating – it was even worse than when Vile had been holding his hand.

"Oh," said Witch Wormwood, "so it wasn't the hag, then? Or are you still cursed?" She peered at Twig, squinting. "You look fine to me, but to be perfectly honest I didn't think you much looked cursed at all when I saw you the first time. I wouldn't have known if Glimfinkle hadn't explained it all to me. Very helpful, for a gnome. Of course, it's been years since I've seen a curse that had to be broken with true love's kiss. They're not that common any more, not like in my youth. No romance in the world today. I was surprised Ripplemintz even sent you to see me. Everyone knows there's only one way out of that one. I hope the mints helped."

Twig let out a strangled sound that was something between someone squeezing a cat and a hiccoughing goose. Witch Wormwood pounded him on the back.

"What . . . what exactly did Glimfinkle tell you my curse was?" he asked.

"Oh, he wasn't terribly specific," Witch Wormwood said lightly. "Said you'd run afoul of an angry fairy godmother . . . Something about bad breath and skinny knees and not being able to grow any muscles . . ." The witch's voice trailed off as she peered at him again, a bit uncomfortably. "Oh, you *haven't* broken the curse, have you? I'm so sorry, and me going on and on about it." She patted Twig on the shoulder. "I've got more mints, if you like. That's what I won this for," she said, pointing proudly to the ribbon pinned to her dress. "They've got dragon mint in them, so they're extra strong."

Twig couldn't even think what to say, but what he did know was that he was going to dropkick that ridiculous gnome if he ever saw him again. What if Witch Wormwood had been able to help him right in the beginning? He could have been sitting at home right now having a lie down after reading a good book. It was a good thing Vile wasn't with him. Or Glimfinkle. Someone would probably be getting choked. Or hexed, if her hagging was working.

No, Vile must never find out. He felt himself turn red just thinking about it.

Witch Wormwood cleared her throat and fidgeted a bit from foot to foot. "Anyway, were you planning to catch the final elimination round before the wizard duels begin? It's bound to be a good one. They're down to three young whippersnappers from Aramore going up against the king's chief wizard, Pumice Pummelstone. He's offered to take them all on at once. Always puts on a good show, that one. Have you watched any of the other elimination rounds?"

"No." Twig finally managed to choke out some actual words. "Actually, I'm entered in the competition for Muckwood." Just saying that out loud made him flush hot, then cold. He had the feeling he probably looked like clotted cream and strawberries all mashed together.

"Oh, really? They sent you instead of Ripplemintz? Didn't even know Muckwood took part in the contest . . ."

"Er . . ." He took a deep breath and explained the real reason he'd come to see her originally and a condensed version of everything that had happened since then and why he'd been sent to compete.

Witch Wormwood stared at him a long moment and shook her head. "A curse isn't your problem at all," she said finally.

Twig sighed. "Is it something you could have helped with or not?"

"What do *you* think?" she asked.

Twig didn't even have to think about it. "No," he said.

"Now you're thinking," the witch said. "Good thing too, if you're going up against wizards like Pummelstone and Kudzu. They're at least three times your age, boy, and with all the experience that goes along with that. And let's not even talk about the wizards like Sumac."

"So you think I should drop out of the competition?"

"I didn't say that," she said, eyebrows raised. "Magic is as magic does, and if your magic is as powerful as you say, then you've got a chance. Besides, I do know King Mervyn. If you disobey a direct order from him, you'd better have a darn good reason or a good horse to get away on. Of course, you could always turn him into a frog."

Twig hadn't considered that as an option before. "Really? The king?"

Wormwood cackled, that proper witchy cackle that made him jump. "I wouldn't recommend it. If you think you don't want to handle the responsibility of being the most powerful wizard in the world, you certainly don't want to lead a hostile takeover of a kingdom."

The witch had a point. Twig sighed. Things had been a lot less complicated when he'd just been Twig Thicket.

Dearest Twig,

Given that you are by far the least experienced wizard to ever compete at the Euphonium, I didn't think it too out of line to provide you with a few helpful tips. Make of it what you will and good luck. The only way forwards is through!

— Witch Wormwood

This should be obvious, but keep your eye on your opponent.

Don't duel on an empty stomach. But don't eat too much either. You don't want to get sick in front of everyone or pass out.

Wear clean underwear.

Tansy of Humble probably won't try to kill you but don't expect her to go easy on you either just because you're young. She's straightforward and no-nonsense.

Sumac Crabapple is one to worry about. Don't get distracted by his boils and do not underestimate him. If he can get away with it, he'll cheat somehow. He doesn't play by the rules.

Pumice Pummelstone is a show off, but very powerful. He'll always try to cast first and he's out to impress the crowd.

Stix of Loudwater is past his prime and hasn't won at the Euphonium in years. That said, he's got a wicked way with lightning, so watch the skies.

Kudzu of The Spire is generally non-lethal but overwhelming. He's really got a green thumb, so I hope you aren't allergic to anything.

Dill of Stonelake has no imagination and he's slow on the draw, but he's also built like an ogre, so he's hard to knock over with brute strength.

Pyrite of Goldlocke hates to lose and he always wants to be the best. He's not the best wizard out there, but he is the most ambitious, other than Sumac Crabapple. He's half-dwarf and loves anything gold.

Burdock of Blessing has never won. He specialises in water magic, so unless they ever move the Euphonium to the water, you don't have to worry about him.

Chert of Rockpool is a decent sort. He only competes because the king makes him. He's never made it past the first round, so I wouldn't worry about him.

Hemp of Dunmire is known for his intricate spells, but they aren't really suitable for duelling. So if you can get off the first spell, you should have no problem.

Wendell of Elder is a quarter elven, a quarter satyr, and possibly part dryad. I'm not even sure he's part human. He tends to cast very aggressive spells, so be sure to have a shield ready.

Corm of Waterdown ... honestly, I don't know much about him. He's only been the resident wizard for two years and didn't compete in the Euphonium last year. He's quite young, but still at least eight years older than you.

Stem of Frost is rumoured to be part frost giant. He's certainly very tall and he prefers ice and cold spells. You can easily take him out with a well-placed fireball or two. He can't stand Salamar of The Burning Islands for obvious reasons.

Nance of Justice was a noble knight before he discovered he had a talent for magic. He's still more comfortable with a sword than a wand, though, so just attack him with something showy if you go up against him.

Coal of Kindle is very tall.
That's all I know about him.

18

IN WHICH THINGS ARE
ELIMINATED

Witch Wormwood looked him up and down and seemed to come to a decision. "Come on, boy, you might as well get a look at the competition. Maybe then you won't get turned into a toad. Power only gets you so far, you know. There's a lot more to being a wizard and surviving the Euphonium than just that."

She led the way to the duelling pitch in the centre of the Euphonium, all the while regaling Twig with tales of past duels. For a witch, she seemed remarkably well-informed about wizards. Twig remembered what Ripplemintz had said about her being a big gossip. She certainly knew which wizards cheated on their spell casting and which didn't. Pyrite of the Kingdom of Goldlocke was apt to cast early and apologize later and Pumice was known as Quick-Spell. Some people said that Stix of Loudwater had made a pact with demonic spirits. And she warned him not to be distracted by Sumac's boils, but that was a hazard Twig had already experienced.

"You do know how this works, don't you, boy?"

Twig debated for a moment about whether or not he should admit his lack of knowledge and decided it was best to just be honest. "Not really," he answered.

Wormwood sighed. "Well, hopefully you do know that each kingdom has a resident wizard, yes? Like Ripplemintz, except better." Twig nodded. "They are the king's champion in magical matters, so to speak. However, there are generally other wizards who might want to have a go at competing for glory at the Euphonium and, perhaps, even impressing their king. So they come to compete as well but only one wizard can compete for each kingdom in the end. Thus there are the elimination rounds where hopefuls duel until only one wizard remains per kingdom."

That was why the wizard at the registration hut had said he'd go straight through and had a place. No one else was here for Muckwood.

"The other elimination rounds have all been settled, except for Aramore's. They saved the best for last. Aramore's chock full of wizards and they all want a taste of the pie. You'd do well to remember that."

The pitch was well surrounded with spectators, but Witch Wormwood pushed her way through with judicious use of her bony elbows. She got them right up to the wooden fence that ringed the pitch, directly across from the raised platform that the three judges sat on. Twig tried to get a good look at them without seeming like he was staring. Two were really old and almost comically tiny, with long beards and ornately embroidered silken robes. They looked like Ripplemintz would probably look in another ten or fifteen years, Twig decided. The third was younger, though still old enough to have grey sprinkled through his dark, curled hair. His skin had a deep red

tinge, like a fire that had burned long and hot.

"Who are they?" he finally asked, pointing.

Witch Wormwood snorted. "Ripplemintz really hasn't been teaching you anything, has he? That lazy sot. The venerable Haggis of Aramore is on the left. He's the one with the longest beard. Back in his day, he won the Euphonium ten years running! As you can see, that was some time ago. No one's broken his record since. On the right is Moss Milkweed, who never settled in a kingdom but instead travelled the land righting wrongs and things like that. He's known as the People's Wizard."

"I've heard of him," said Twig, a little defensively. *Everyone* had heard of the People's Wizard. Twig hadn't known that he was still alive, though. His great gran had told him about seeing Milkweed when she was a young girl. He had to be ancient now.

"Good for you," said Witch Wormwood before carrying on. "The one in the middle is Salamar from the Burning Islands. Some say he's half efreet. Now, I don't know about that, but I've seen the man duel before and he's a master of fire, that's for sure. Lucky for you he's a judge and not a contestant this year."

Twig hadn't heard of Salamar before, but he had heard of the Burning Islands. They lay between the Midden – where trolls and goblins called home – and the volcano off the coast, called the Eye of the Sea. The sea boiled there, or so people said.

"Oh, and here come the contestants!" called Witch Wormwood.

"Did any of the official wizards get unseated this year?" asked Twig.

Witch Wormwood cackled again. Twig really wished she wouldn't do that. It kept making the hairs on the back of his neck stand up. "That hasn't happened in a good many years," the witch said, patting him on the head – which he also wished she wouldn't do. "I daresay you are the youngest and least-prepared wizard to have *ever* completed in the Euphonium."

Twig took an inadvertent step backwards, but the crowd pushed him back immediately. Witch Wormwood grinned at him, though it didn't make him feel any better.

There was a spattering of half-hearted applause from the crowd as three youngish wizards entered from the left side of the pitch. They looked around Badger's age or maybe a bit younger, but they were definitely all *much* older than Twig. The clapping swelled into a roar as Pumice Pummelstone entered from the other side, his red cloak sweeping behind him. He was a large, well-built man with broad shoulders and the kind of swaggering walk that meant he knew what a fine figure he cut. He carried a wand in his right hand and wore a courtier's doublet underneath his cloak, rather than normal wizard robes. He could have been a nobleman with those fancy robes. A woman next to Twig fanned herself and sighed loudly as she looked at him.

"Showboat," said Witch Wormwood with a grin.

"Watch the wand, boy."

It was unusual for a wizard to use a wand – most wizards used staffs, if anything, though some used nothing at all. Ripplemintz had a wooden ruler that he kept up his sleeve.

The three young wizards all looked very nervous, but they stepped up to the bare patch of earth that marked their end of the pitch. It was a bit scorched, as if someone earlier had been incinerated there. Twig didn't ask if that was actually the case.

Pumice waved his way to stand on the opposite patch of dirt. He stopped, wand held nonchalantly off to the side. He bowed to the three now terrified looking wizards and they bowed back. There was a sharp whistle and Salamar the judge raised a hand as everyone looked at him. "On my signal," he said, in a deep voice that rang over the whole pitch.

Twig focused on Pumice. Would he have to duel him later? It was possible, if he lasted that long. Pummelstone still held his wand loosely in his hand, but Twig could tell that he was ready; the tip of it twitched, ever so slightly.

"That's right, boy, don't take your eyes off him," said Witch Wormwood. "He'll have prepared something big, mark my words."

Salamar's hand descended sharply to mark the start of the match. Before his arm was even all the way down, Pumice had whipped his wand around in a tight, controlled circle. Twig didn't catch the words he spoke – the crowd was too loud – but he saw the effect: a snake-like beam of light erupted from the wand and hurtled towards the three wizards. One of them fumbled his staff and dropped it as he attempted to cast some kind of spell, but the other two completely froze. The beam twined itself about their feet, and Pumice raised the tip of the wand so that they were upended in the air. As they dangled from their ankles, their robes, as gravity demanded, fell, covering their flailing arms and faces and leaving their pale skinny legs and not entirely hole-free underpants open to the public. The crowd roared with laughter.

Pumice took a bow. Then he twitched his wand in a short, sharp motion and the three wizards fell in one big tangled heap.

"Make sure you wear clean underwear if you come up against Pummelstone," Witch Wormwood cackled, elbowing Twig in the ribs.

The Basics of Duelling

1. Absolutely no spellcasting before the match, including glamours.

2. Wands, staffs and well-behaved familiars (no larger than a medium-sized leprechaun) are allowed.

3. Non-magical pointy weapons and armour are strictly prohibited.

4. Upon taking your position in the pitch, signal your readiness by bowing to your opponent.

5. Wait for the signal from the officiating wizard before casting.

6. No maiming or injuring of spectators, except by unavoidable accident.

7. You must completely remove all bits of your opponent from the mound to win the match.

8. No illegal spellcasting.

9. No toilet breaks.

10. Please try not to kill anyone.

For full guidelines, please refer to Sap Duckweed's
The Wizard's Complete Duelling Guidebook &
History of the Kingdoms, Volumes 1 through 12.

19

IN WHICH IT BEGINS
WITH A MUMBLE

"That was it?!" exclaimed Twig. Witch Wormwood patted him on the head again. It *still* didn't make him feel any better.

He watched with sick fascination as the three young wizards scurried off the pitch with red faces. A few people pelted them with tomatoes as they went, which seemed a bit much to Twig. After all, they'd just shown their holey underwear to everyone. It wasn't like they needed any more embarrassment.

Salamar stood to address the crowd. "That concludes the elimination rounds for Aramore." He waved a majestic hand in the air and there was a flash of light and an answering show of sparks from a bulletin board near to the judging stand as parchment scrolls appeared pinned to it. "The full schedule has now been posted. The first round of duels will commence tomorrow morning promptly at cock's crow."

"Shall we go see?" asked Witch Wormwood. "I hope you're not the first to go on the chopping block. I'm not a morning person, you know."

They fought their way through the crowd again, Twig feeling a bit like a minnow trying to swim upstream. Not even Witch Wormwood's elbows were giving them much of an advantage, as everyone was heading in the same direction. And Twig suddenly realized that he was hungry. It seemed forever since he'd eaten anything.

"Create a path or feel my wrath," he muttered under his breath, and he waved his hand back and forth, perhaps using a slightly bigger swoop than he'd intended. The people in front of them parted like grain hit by a scythe, though luckily in not quite so final a fashion. They were simply shoved to the side until a clear swath

appeared leading straight to the noticeboard.

"Well, well, well," said Witch Wormwood with an appreciative nod. "I see you weren't kidding about the power, at any rate."

"Er, sorry," said Twig to the confused people around them, as he quickly scurried down the cleared path. "Pardon me, sorry. Excuse me. Coming through. Sorry about the trouble."

"Oh, stop *apologizing*," said a familiar voice. Vile stepped into view, standing by the board. She pointed to it with a huge half-gnawed turkey leg she was holding in her hand. "You're up against Tansy of Humble tomorrow at noon."

"Tansy?" asked Twig.

"That's interesting," said Witch Wormwood, rubbing her chin. "She's one of the few female wizards in the kingdoms that I know of. Definitely the only one that competes at the Euphonium."

"A woman?"

"That *is* what female means," said Vile. "At least, it was the last time I checked." She took a big bite out of the turkey leg and grinned at him, bits of turkey and grease everywhere, including on her face. Perhaps she had forgiven him for their last conversation. Or maybe she was just happy to be insulting him again.

Witch Wormwood elbowed him. She did have very sharp elbows. "Maybe it's just as well your curse wasn't what I thought it was," she said, giving him an exaggerated wink.

"What?" asked Vile.

"Nothing," said Twig quickly. He thought it best to change the subject and he had something important on his mind anyway. "Where did you get that food? I'm starving."

"Here," said Vile. She dug into her bag and pulled out another turkey leg. Twig took it gingerly and inspected it. It looked relatively unscathed. He took an experimental sniff. It smelled good. In fact, his mouth immediately started watering. He'd have to chance it and hope that it hadn't been next to anything horrible in Vile's bag. He suspected she kept toads in there, but he didn't want to think about that. He ate a bite and then another.

Witch Wormwood watched them both, a small,

quiet smile on her face.

"I don't suppose you two have any place to stay for the night, do you?" the witch asked. "Likely didn't think that far ahead, I imagine. Follow me."

Twig and Vile looked at each other. They hadn't really thought about anything beyond reaching the Euphonium.

"Are you sure?" asked Twig.

Witch Wormwood's grin got bigger. She made to elbow Twig again but he moved out of the way before the witch made contact. "I like you, Twig Thicket. You just might have a chance in this thing," she said. "First, I'm going to get you two settled and then I'm going to find my bookie."

Witch Wormwood took them to her double-decker

caravan house parked outside the Euphonium in a ring of other witch wagons. It looked a lot like her normal wooden house in the Withering Swamp, but it was on wheels instead of stilts and had five chimneys. It seemed to run on steam power and witch ingenuity, with a bubbling cauldron under each chimney which made the inside feel warm and hazy and slightly like they were swimming in soup.

Twig borrowed a supply of paper, spelled himself a pencil from a branch and set to work on some rhyming spells to memorize ahead of his duel the next day. The other wizards had been preparing for the Euphonium for *months*. He had a night. Vile watched him for a while before declaring it all too boring. She took herself off shopping.

While she was gone, Twig had a go at prising some advice out of Witch Wormwood, as she seemed more helpful than not now that he understood why she hadn't even tried to help him before.

"Should I try to get off the first spell?" he asked. Pumice had certainly outmatched his opponents on that point.

"Depends on who you're up against. Sometimes it's better to respond and then quick-fire something else. It also depends on *you*. Do you think you're the kind of wizard who fires first and asks questions later?"

Twig couldn't answer that. He'd never duelled anyone before. Could he attack someone who hadn't attacked him first?

Witch Wormwood poured him some tea. "You should play to your own strengths," she said. "Certainly, you have to worry about what they're going to do, but be true to yourself. If you're not, you'll hesitate. And he who hesitates . . ."

". . . is lost," finished Twig. He'd definitely heard that before. But what *were* his strengths?

"Anyway, I'd start off preparing some standard spells that you know you'll likely need. Like a shield, for one. You're *definitely* going to need a shield."

At least he'd had some practice with that because of Vile and Glimfinkle.

"So . . . have you ever heard of a hag losing her

hagging for any reason without being cursed or hexed or anything?"

Witch Wormwood looked at him in surprise. She put a finger alongside her button of a nose and looked thoughtful. "Hm, no, can't say as I have. But that kind of thing usually sorts itself out, you know. Once a hag, always a hag, that's what I always say." She leaned over the table and looked uncomfortably deep into Twig's eyes. "Why do you ask?"

"No reason," he said, looking away, and went back to scribbling his rhymes.

Vile came back soon after that and he studiously did not look at Witch Wormwood. He shouldn't have asked. It was Vile's business, anyway. He had his own stuff to worry about. Namely, not getting killed.

Vile went to sleep almost immediately, after showing him her haul of spider's knees and chocolate-covered chokecherries, but then *she* didn't have a duel coming up. She was still insisting that she wasn't going to compete in the hag scrap but Twig suspected she really wanted to. He caught her trying to hex one of Witch Wormwood's toads. It didn't go well. The poor thing *lost* warts instead of gaining them, but on the other hand, that was sort of progress – at least *something* had happened. Vile had lost a few more warts herself. Twig wondered if he should try to remove the spell or let it wear off on its own, as it seemed to be doing. Some things were better left alone.

He and Vile spent the next morning practising, which mostly involved her throwing random things at him and him trying to not get hit. Witch Wormwood even loaned them some angry toads and rodents of unusual size, after she made him promise not to explode them.

Before Twig knew it, it was noon and he was awaiting his turn outside the duelling pitch, accompanied by Vile and Witch Wormwood. There had been no sign of Glimfinkle or Beaky.

Some white-robed wizards were carrying out Hemp of Dunmire, covered in something green and otherwise indescribable that Sumac Crabapple had defeated him with. It smelled a lot like the innards of Sumac's boil. Twig's stomach twisted.

Twig had never seen a female wizard before.

There weren't any specific rules or laws about it but, somehow, most women who were inclined to magic became witches. Ripplemintz said it didn't really matter what you called yourself, it was about your commitment to magic. He was probably the only wizard who thought that, however.

Tansy was a tall woman about the same age as Twig's mum, but that was where all resemblance ended. She was whippet thin and very neatly dressed, without a hair out of place. That's not to say she was finely clothed; her robes were serviceable at best and not at all fancy. Her brown hair was tied back in a plait that went all the way down her back and reached her knees. She didn't have a staff or a wand, Twig noticed, but she did have a bracelet twined about her arm that looked like a red lizard, with its tail wound up past her elbow. She looked more like an oracle than the actual oracle did.

Vile clapped him on the back. "Ready, Twig?"

He wanted to say no, but instead he said, "Yes."

"Remember," said the wizard who let him on to the pitch, "death is frowned upon."

Twig thought that death should be quite a bit more

than just frowned upon.

"Branch of Muckwood," announced an officiating wizard, who had earlier introduced himself as Root of Aramore. He waved Twig forwards with a bored sweep of his hand.

"Er, Twig," said Twig, perhaps a bit more querulously than he had intended.

Root stared at him. "No, that's not right at all. Weren't you listening? My name is Root, boy." He waved Twig on again, this time impatiently.

Twig slowly walked out to the same spot that the three wizards had stood when they were embarrassed by Pumice Pummelstone. It was a small dirt mound, freshly raked to get rid of the green goo from the previous match. He felt very exposed and wished he had a staff or a wand or anything other than the now rather worse-for-wear bag that Ripplemintz had given him. There wasn't really anything useful in it, but he'd kept it slung over his shoulder for comfort. His cloak, at least, floated out behind him. He'd refreshed it with some new clouds that morning and it waved crisply in the small breeze.

The small crowd was quiet. It wasn't even a quarter of the size of the audience that had turned out for Pumice's match. Obviously, no one expected much to happen. Twig rather hoped they were right. Some of the people (mostly hags) had even left after Sumac's match.

Vile began whooping, her fist pumping the air. "Go, Twig!" she shouted. "Woot, woot!" Twig ducked his head down but squared his shoulders.

Tansy bowed to Twig and he bowed to her, trying to keep one eye on Salamar. The fire wizard was staring at him curiously. Probably, Twig thought, wondering what in the kingdoms he was doing there. Tansy looked very far away but somehow also very close. She also looked like she knew what she was doing.

Salamar's hand fell in what felt like slow motion.

Tansy raised her arm and murmured something that Twig couldn't hear. Her lizard bracelet leapt off her arm, growing as it did until it reached the ground. It was about the size of a large salamander which, Twig now saw, was exactly what it was. It burst into flames and streaked towards him at a dead run.

All the spells that Twig had memorized flew out of his head. All his panicked brain could think was *salamander*!

"Um ... uh, *Salamander, Pomander*!" he shouted out, not even bothering to make any fancy hand movements or do anything flashy.

The fiery salamander transformed into a clove-studded orange mid-leap, and rolled to a stop at his feet, letting off a lovely aroma that reminded him of winter evenings sitting around the hearth at the Thicket home. Twig took a deep breath. So much for Tansy being non-lethal. His heart was thudding.

"Sparky!" shouted Tansy, looking stunned. This was Twig's chance. He had to take it.

> *"Tansy of Humble*
> *Your mind's a jumble,*
> *You can only mumble*
> *And bumble about!"*

It wasn't elegant and Twig had completely forgotten the second verse he'd come up with the night before, but the spell flew from his fingers with a cascade of sparks. Tansy opened her mouth to cast a spell in return but it was too late. The spell had hit her and nothing intelligible came out. She looked confused and tried to speak again, but then a butterfly flew by and she wandered off to follow it.

There was silence around the pitch for a few moments as the crowd watched Tansy stumble around after the butterfly. Then she sat down abruptly and started counting her fingers and toes.

"You did it, Twig!" yelled Vile.

Witch Wormwood clapped loudly and, after a bit, other people in the small crowd gathered around did as well. It was very surprised-sounding applause.

"And the winner is . . . Twig Thicket of Muckwood!" announced Salamar in his booming voice. He sounded surprised too.

241

20

IN WHICH THERE ARE FEWER WARTS BUT TOO MANY BOILS

Twig was still reeling from having actually won as Vile and Witch Wormwood dragged him back to the witch's caravan. "I actually did it," he kept saying to himself, not even realizing he was saying it out loud.

"Yes," said Vile, as she kicked open the door, "so you've said. About twenty times."

"And a right good job of it you did, too," said Glimfinkle, making Twig jump. He was seated on Witch Wormwood's table, holding a gold coin in one hand with the other placed protectively on a bulging pouch that looked to be holding more of them. Vile groaned when she saw him.

"Where've you been?" asked Twig, surprised out of his reverie.

"Had some thinkin' to do," said the gnome.

"And betting too, from the looks of it," said Witch Wormwood, coming in behind them.

Glimfinkle gave the witch a sly wink. "Same as ye," he said. "It was yer bookie told me where to find ye. I figured if ye were betting on the boy, I ought to as well."

"Speaking of which," said the witch, "I've got an errand to run. I'll leave you to it." And with that, she was gone.

"Where's Beaky?" asked Vile.

"Ah, he's off somewhere. Said he was hungry somethin' wicked. Besides, he don't really approve of me bettin'."

"You really bet on me?" asked Twig.

"Aye, I did," said the gnome. "And I've got some coin on the wee hag too."

"What?" said Vile sharply. She laughed, but it didn't sound at all like she was amused. "Well, you've lost that bet. I'm not even competing in the hag scrap."

"Wot?" shouted Glimfinkle. "But I saw yer name on the list! Don't be tellin' me there's another hag named Vile out there!"

"In case you hadn't noticed," said Vile, stomping around the table, "I haven't been able to cast a curse in ages! And don't think I haven't tried! You should be covered in pus and boils, you little runt!"

Glimfinkle jumped up and did some stomping of his own. "Well, that's just perfect, that is! Ye could've told me!"

"*AAAARRRrrrrrrgggggghhhhh!*" Vile kicked an iron cauldron and then jumped up and down holding her foot. "Ow! My toe!"

"Serves ye right, ye frabnactious hag! I hope ye broke it!"

"Stop it right now! Both of you!" shouted Twig. Sparks shot from his fingers, though he hadn't even cast a spell. At least it got their attention. He shot a look at Vile, who was glaring at him. "Sit down!" he ordered. "I mean it."

They both sat, but it was

obviously under protest.

"What is wrong with you two?" Twig asked, but then he held up his hands when they both started to reply at once. "No, never mind, forget I asked." He sat down too. The *duel* hadn't exhausted him, but *they* certainly did. "For better or worse—"

"—Worse," mumbled Vile.

"—We're in this together. The three of us. We've been through so much—"

"—Yer bloomin' fault," muttered Glimfinkle.

"—And we should stick together and support each other." Twig took a deep breath. "Even if some of us are lying little scoundrels." He pointed at the gnome in case it wasn't clear who he was talking about. The gnome did his best to look shocked at the accusation. "Don't you pull that face at me," said Twig. "I talked to Witch Wormwood and she told me everything."

"About what?" asked Vile.

Twig blushed. "Nothing important," he said. "Doesn't matter now, anyway; the point is, we're in this together."

"What's that gnome ever done for me?" asked Vile.

"He doesn't even like me!"

"He just bet on you, didn't he?" said Twig.

"So?"

"Do you think he'd have bet on you if he didn't think you were going to win?"

"I . . ." Vile bit back what she'd been about to say and turned instead to the gnome. "You thought I could win?"

Glimfinkle shifted back and forth. "Well, yeah. Yer annoying and a right pain in the bupkiss, but yer the best wee hag I've ever known." As he spoke, he grimaced like it pained him to admit it. "And I've known a few hags, trust me. Me second wife, for one."

"Oh," said Vile.

"And the odds are quite long, ye see," the gnome continued. Twig glared at him. Glimfinkle really didn't know when to shut up, but Vile didn't seem to have noticed.

"I'm sorry you've lost your money," she said.

"He doesn't have to," said Twig.

"What do ye mean?" asked Glimfinkle. "Can ye turn Bennie the bookie into a frog fer me? He's a quarter bog troll, so he's nearly there as it is."

"No!" said Twig. "That's not what I meant." He stole a look at Vile. She was staring down at the table. It was time for him to come clean. He twitched his fingers and put up a protective shield just in case. He'd been practising that one and could do it without saying anything at all now. "I think that maybe, just maybe, when I, um, un-mouseified Vile, that might possibly have been the moment when she lost her hagging." He ducked his head reflexively.

"Wot?" said Glimfinkle.

"What?" said Vile. Now she was paying attention.

Twig's fingers twitched again. He explained his suspicions about how her outward vileness seemed to be tied to her inward hagging ability. "And," he concluded, "as you've been losing your, er, ugliness I think you've been getting your hagginess back. Kind of. I think. Maybe."

Vile's fingers were twitching too, Twig noticed. He was pretty sure she was hexing him purely by reflex. It probably wouldn't have done anything, but he was glad he'd put up the shield all the same.

"Well, then," shouted Glimfinkle, jumping to his

feet, "make her pretty again! What're you waitin' fer?"

"Hags aren't pretty," said Vile by rote, like she'd said it a hundred times before.

"Yes, they are," said Twig, taking a deep breath. "Because you *are* a hag and you're pretty." He concentrated and waved both hands in the air in a half-arc around her before she could start arguing.

> *"You've been vile*
> *For awhile,*
> *Now it's time*
> *With this rhyme*
> *To just be YOU."*

Twig hoped it would work. He'd worked on it the night before when he should have been coming up with more spells for the duel.

Rather than a shower of sparks, it was almost as if a small summery breeze left his fingertips. It carried with it the smell of grass and sunshine as it swirled around Vile. It gently blew her wild hair back from her face. She let out a surprised giggle, like it tickled. When everything finally settled, all of Vile's warts were gone and her teeth were whole and white again. Well, whitish. The various layers of dirt and even the leaves caught in her brilliant red hair were still there, because that was who she was. It suited her. Twig spelled up a hand mirror from a cup of water on the table and handed it to her. She took it automatically and stared at her face for a long moment. He couldn't tell if she was pleased or not.

"Come here, gnome," she said, putting down the mirror and grabbing Glimfinkle.

The gnome struggled. "Don't ye dare, ye wicked hag! I've got me face just the way I like it!"

Vile laughed and wiggled her fingers in his face. Then she turned him so he could see the mostly wart-less toad sitting in a cage on Witch Wormwood's counter. She jabbed her fingers at it in a motion that Twig was now *very* familiar with. He held his breath.

The toad jumped as warts POP! POP! popped up all over its plump green body. "Ribbbbiitttt!" it said, though Twig couldn't tell if it was pleased

or upset or merely startled.

"It worked!" said Twig and Vile together, Twig trying not to sound surprised.

"Of course it did," said Glimfinkle. "Yer the world's greatest wizard, ye know!"

Vile insisted they go back out into the Euphonium. She had a large number of people she wanted to curse, feeling that they had cheated her on her shopping trip the day before, which may or may not have been true. Twig agreed to the excursion, as it was good to see her happy about something, even if it was just the possibility of giving people warts, hives and unscratchable itches. Glimfinkle came along as well, jingling his pouch of gold.

For perhaps the first time, it felt like they weren't in a rush or a panic. Twig's next duel wasn't until the following day and he felt pretty comfortable with the spells he'd already worked up. He practised a few as they walked, taking his bubble-like shield up and down and periodically tossing fireballs into the air. That also helped clear a path through the crowd as everyone gave them an extra-wide berth.

Glimfinkle, in a surprisingly generous mood, was freely spending his winnings on treats for everyone and they were all soon stuffed full of unicorn milk ice cream (which was really quite good, though it did tend to give you hiccups), barbecued frog legs served on a stick, and rainbow candyfloss made from actual rainbows by entrepreneurial leprechauns. Vile said that selling so much of it was where they *really* got their gold from.

They were on their way to the amusements to try their hand at the dragon egg shy when their path was blocked by a dark, forbidding figure. Sumac Crabapple, dressed in so many layers of black that he seemed to suck up the sun, stood in their way. But even the wizard's voluminous cape couldn't hide the monstrously huge boils that Vile's parting shot had given him. They made him look like a very angry diseased frog. The one on his nose had grown to be *even bigger* than before. The crowd around them rapidly cleared without any fireball encouragement.

"So," sneered Sumac, "we meet again, Twig Thicket, *boy* wizard." He spat Twig's name like it tasted foul in his mouth. "I saw you won your match against that weakling Tansy with a stupid little party trick."

"Party trick?" said Vile. "I'll show you a party trick—" But Twig grabbed her hand as she raised it, sensing the pent-up magic Sumac was holding in his clenched fist. It felt wicked and dangerous and full of anger, like he'd been holding on to it for a while. The wizard was obviously looking for an excuse to do something horrible.

"What do you want, Sumac?" asked Twig.

The wizard looked disappointed that Twig had stopped Vile from cursing him. So did Vile and Glimfinkle. "Nothing, boy," he said. He smiled, which made the carbuncle on his nose bob up and down. "I just wanted to tell you that I look forward to meeting you on the pitch. If you make it that far, that is. You're up against Pyrite next and he's no pushover."

Twig had heard of Pyrite of Goldlocke – everyone had, even people in Muckwood.

"Meh," said Glimfinkle. "Twig's the world's greatest wizard, ye big gobermouch. He'll beat Pyrite and anyone else wot comes up against 'im, ye included. I stake my coin on it! '

"I'll take that bet," said Sumac. Twig had a bad feeling in his stomach all of a sudden that he suspected wasn't just from too much candyfloss. Sumac spat in his hand and held it out for Glimfinkle to shake. The gnome did the same, albeit with much less spit. Twig winced at the squelching sound their handshake made.

Sumac gave them one last nasty grin, like he knew something they definitely didn't know and it pleased him greatly, then pushed past them and disappeared into the crowd, which opened and closed around him like he was a bit of walking plague.

"Ye better wipe the ground with that piece o' work," said Glimfinkle.

"Let me curse him for you," said Vile, flexing her fingers.

"I won't cheat," said Twig. "And you're going to be busy at the hag scrap, aren't you? It starts tomorrow."

"Yeh!" said Glimfinkle. "I got money on it!"

"Besides," said Twig, thoughtfully, "I don't think you could fit any more boils on him."

21

IN WHICH THERE IS A HAGGING

Twig's duel with Pyrite was scheduled for after breakfast, right around the same time as the hag scrap was scheduled to begin, though the hag scrap often started late as hags weren't generally morning people. Too many late nights spent cackling, apparently.

Beaky flew in just in time to gulp down three helpings of breakfast in very non-magpie fashion. Witch Wormwood served them up a heaping platter of toad sausage (it had a tendency to hop about the plate), scrambled eggs of unknown provenance, and mostly unburnt toast. Twig caught Vile trying to stick some mushrooms on her face with jam when she didn't think he was looking.

"Would you quit it?" he said, knocking one off her cheek. "Just stop. It doesn't matter what you *look* like. It matters what you *do*."

Vile furtively wiped the jam off her face with a napkin – it was possibly the first time in her life she'd used one on purpose. "What if the oracle's right, though?" she said quietly.

"Warts don't make a hag," said Twig firmly. "And that oracle was utter rubbish."

"What exactly did the oracle tell you, anyway?" asked Witch Wormwood, pouring Vile another steaming cup of strong black tea.

"She said I'd never be a proper hag like my gran," said Vile.

"That's not right. She said" – Twig put on a high falsetto voice that didn't actually sound like the oracle at all – "*One cannot be what one is not. You are what you are what you are.*" Twig grimaced. "Whatever that means."

"Hmmmm," said Witch Wormwood. "That does sound like an oracle kind of thing to say, doesn't it? And what about you, Twig?"

"She didn't answer my question at all!" said Twig, stabbing a bit of egg. The whole thing still rankled.

"To be fair, that's not entirely true," said Glimfinkle. "She said yer question was stupid, but you were gettin' the same answer as wot she gave the wee hag no matter what. And me too. Three fer the price of one." He grunted. "No one's ever made any coin that way, did they? Bit suspicious."

"She didn't even charge us," said Twig. "I'm not even sure she's really the oracle."

"Oh, she probably was," said Witch Wormwood knowingly. "You'll just have to wait and see how things shake out. That's the way these things go. Now, then, off with you both. It's time."

"Good luck," said Twig and Vile to each other at the same time.

Glimfinkle and Beaky, looking a bit larger since breakfast, went off with Vile, ostensibly to lend support but probably to make sure she actually competed in the hag scrap. Witch Wormwood went along with Twig.

"If you've seen one hag scrap, you've seen them

all," she confided once they had parted ways with the gnome and Vile. "Besides, hags aren't known for their aim *or* their discretion. Half of the spectators wind up with hives for days. And," the witch added, "it'll be going on for ages. We can go see how she's doing after you win your duel."

Twig wished he was as confident in himself as the witch was in him, but Sumac had worried him. Pyrite was definitely a wizard to watch out for. His only known weakness was his greed, at least according to the *Wizard Quarterly*. Well, that and his vanity, Twig supposed, but the two were connected. Pyrite had been voted Best Dressed Wizard of the Euphonium *every year*. It was one of the reasons Ripplemintz never went. He'd made his own robe out of phoenix feathers one year but Pyrite had bewitched some silk worms into spinning a robe so fine it felt like air. Twig had seen Ripplemintz's feather one; it looked a bit like a bedraggled chicken. He privately suspected they hadn't really been phoenix feathers at all.

There were significantly more spectators

waiting to watch the second round of duels. When they finally reached the entry on to the pitch, Twig grew even more concerned. Sumac was on the opposite side having a cozy little chat with Pyrite. They looked like night and day, evil and good or, more likely, evil and gaudy. Where Sumac was in his customary black, Pyrite's robe was so gold it glittered. It actually hurt to look at him when he stepped out of the shade of the tent and into the sun.

Even worse than the fact that they were together was that they were looking his way and nodding in agreement. Sumac passed Pyrite something, which quickly disappeared into the billowing golden sleeve of his robe.

"Never trust a wizard," said Witch Wormwood darkly. She had noticed the exchange too.

"Hey!" said Twig after a moment, realizing what he'd just heard.

"Present company excepted," the witch said. "For now." She winked at Twig. "Power tends to corrupt, Twig, and you've got an awful lot of power."

"I won't ever be like them," he grumbled. He

didn't even really want to be here, did he? What did Wormwood think he was going to do? Take over the kingdoms? That was something *Sumac* might want, not *him*. Anyone who could kill his own gran for more power was definitely not to be trusted.

"Well," said Witch Wormwood, "looks like it's time. Good luck and watch out. I don't trust Pyrite much further than I can throw him and I've got a bad back. He stiffed me on a bottle of hen's teeth once."

"Er ... thanks," said Twig. He'd hoped the witch might have given him slightly more useful last-minute advice than that.

"Ready, Stick?" asked the Wizard Root, scribbling something on a bit of parchment.

"Twig," said Twig.

"No, I'm *Root*," said Root, looking annoyed.

"I know," said Twig. "*I'm*—"

"Then why'd you call me Twig?"

"Never mind," said Twig, gritting his teeth. "I'm ready." He didn't look at Witch Wormwood, as he suspected she was hiding a smile behind her hands.

"Stick of Muckwood!" announced Root at the top

of his lungs.

Twig swore he heard Sumac snigger from across the pitch. He squared his shoulders and walked out. Pyrite did the same, his arms crossed in front of him and his hands stuck up his sleeves. *What was he hiding?* He definitely had something up his sleeve and it was bound to be no good for Twig. Ripplemintz had always said that there were two kinds of wizards: those who hid things up their sleeves and those who found things there. Twig wasn't entirely sure what that meant really, but he knew his teacher was of the latter variety. He was always finding things he'd lost up his sleeves. In fact, he'd once found a hedgehog that had grown fat on the biscuits that Ripplemintz also stuffed up there.

Pyrite nodded grandly to the crowd. They cheered.

Twig bowed to the crowd. Witch Wormwood let out a gratifying "Whoop whoop!" but that was about it. Everyone else was dead quiet. Pyrite very clearly gave him a jaunty wink, the kind that said a lot of things, none of them very nice.

Twig definitely didn't like Pyrite. Anyone who hung

out with Sumac was suspect anyway, Twig thought to himself. He was so preoccupied with glaring at the wizard that he almost missed the drop of Salamar's hand signalling the beginning of the duel.

Pyrite didn't. He immediately flung a fizzing whizzbanger at Twig, who reflexively threw up his shield. It bounced off not so harmlessly towards the crowd and singed the point of a witch's hat before whizzing off into the cloudless sky.

It hadn't been a particularly strong spell that Pyrite had thrown. Twig's shield was still solid – he could feel it. He waited to see what the wizard would follow up with but Pyrite merely smiled at him and nodded like he was allowing Twig a turn, all the while with his hands once again up his sleeves. Did he have that little respect for Twig that he wasn't even bothering to defend himself? Twig could feel his face turning red.

He flung an answering fireball at Pyrite, twice as big as the spell that the wizard had thrown at him. Pyrite just idly stood there, watching it hurtle towards him. At the very last moment he pulled his hands out of his sleeves but he didn't seem to cast anything. The spell

simply vanished up his right sleeve.

Poof.

Twig felt the magic get swallowed up, and caught a glimpse of a milky white bubble-like ball in Pyrite's grasp before the wizard calmly put his hands back in his sleeves.

The dirty cheat had a spellcatcher! That must have been what Sumac had passed him!

Twig was more familiar than he wanted to be with spellcatchers. Ripplemintz often used them in his experiments in an attempt to keep explosions contained and spells from escaping the tower. They worked pretty well, usually. But they had their limitations. They could only hold so much before they, in turn, exploded, usually causing three times the mess that would have happened to begin with. Twig wasn't very fond of them.

He bit back a grin and commenced flinging spell after spell at Pyrite in quick succession. If he were a betting person like Glimfinkle, he'd bet that Pyrite was wagering he would run out of power and then be easy to finish off. Well, thought Twig, he wasn't going to make it that easy on him.

Twig flung fireballs, snowballs and even whizzing balls of dung at the wizard. And thunder and lightning and rain followed by a hapless barrage of ensorcelled pigeons who happened to be passing by. Then Twig pitched in a sandstorm for good measure. The crowd cheered as Twig kept the spells coming, not pausing to even think about what he was casting. Anything he saw, he threw. Pointy witch's hats, skeins of rainbow candyfloss, and even a gaseous cloud of donkey farts.

Pyrite's smile began to slip as the spells kept coming. Did he know about the failings of spellcatchers? Or did he not expect this much power from someone so young? Twig didn't care. He just kept casting, with his eyes fixed on the wizard across from him.

He'd just cast an exceptionally large bolt of lightning when the spellcatcher finally began to shake and swell inside Pyrite's sleeve. Pyrite now looked more than worried. He tried to keep the now-glowing spellcatcher hidden up his sleeve but, Twig knew from experience, the bubble would be getting hotter and hotter and harder and harder to hold. With a gasp, the wizard dropped it as the spellcatcher exploded with a muffled but emphatic *whumpf*, and Pyrite was blown clear off his feet – and off of the mound itself – his golden robe reduced to tatters and his entire body encrusted and encased in *everything* that Twig had flung at him.

Twig's shield spell held, and he let it go once he was sure the fallout was done. He emerged completely unscathed, which was more than he could say about the first row or two of spectators. They weren't quite as covered in dung and feathers and the like as Pyrite, who lay moaning in a heap on the ground, but they all most decidedly needed a bath. Someone definitely wouldn't be winning Best Dressed Wizard this year.

Twig and Witch Wormwood could tell the hag scrap was still going as they approached the field, by the dazed and wart-ridden people wandering away. The hag scrap wasn't held on a fancy pitch like the wizard duels. For safety reasons, it was in a muddy open area at the very edge of the Euphonium, surrounded by a simple wooden fence that didn't do anything to stop the hexes and curses. It was definitely a "watch at your own risk" event, but that didn't stop a large crowd from gathering. Everyone liked a good hag scrap.

"I don't suppose you could throw up a shield on us, could you?" asked Witch Wormwood. "I don't really fancy any warts."

"Good idea," said Twig. He put up a new, hopefully hex-proof shield around them both – and just in time. He felt more than saw a startled chicken go shooting by him.

"Oi!" said Witch Wormwood. "That's a tough curse to pull off! That's a Henbit Special!" She rubbed her hands together. "Looks like this year's hag scrap is a good one!" She pulled Twig along with her to the fence, shoving a few people out of the way.

Twig had fully expected the field to be full of hags and the air to be full of curses and hexes. But he hadn't expected most of the hags to be flat out on the ground, groaning and covered in more warts and boils and unidentifiable afflictions than he'd *ever* seen in his entire life. He also hadn't expected Vile to be standing in the very middle of the field, arms up and hands outstretched (the fingers on one hand twisted into a warding symbol and the other in a configuration he recognized as what she did when hexing someone with boils), hair frizzed out like she'd been caught in a lightning storm, and the biggest grin he had ever seen on her face as she shouted out curses to the left and right. She was incandescently happy.

"Oh, my," said Witch Wormwood mildly.

There were only four other hags still standing on the field and, as they watched, one of them collapsed under the weight of about thirty quivering putrescent boils that suddenly popped up all over her body. Two of the hags had taken the limp bodies of some of their fallen comrades and had made a makeshift wall that they were cowering behind. Other than Vile, the only hag actually standing up was Nasty. She looked nearly as happy as her sister, even if she was sporting a collection of new purplish warts all over her face.

"Oh, my," Twig agreed. There wasn't really anything else to say.

He jumped as Beaky landed on the fence post next to them with Glimfinkle on his back. The gnome had been circling the field from the relatively safe vantage point of the sky. Beaky looked to have stopped for another snack on the way. He was about the size of an eagle now, but still coloured like a magpie. A few people near them backed away, giving them space to breathe.

Witch Wormwood took a look at the much-larger-than-average magpie and raised an eyebrow at Twig. He shrugged. She grinned and turned back to watch the hagging.

"Ain't Vile somethin'?" the gnome said proudly.

"I've never seen the like."

"I'd always heard the

Hornworts were a force to be reckoned with," said Witch Wormwood, "but I must admit that I hadn't ever imagined carnage quite like this." She rubbed her hands together again with glee. "Excellent hagging, I must say."

Vile and Nasty both advanced towards the two hiding hags. One of them, peeking around the elbow of the hag she was hiding behind, saw them coming and made a run for it.

"Oooh, that was a rookie mistake," said Glimfinkle.

He was right. Vile flung a curse so complicated at the hag's retreating back that it looked like an interpretive dance. The hag sprouted an impressive collection of boils, some putrid and green, others pus-filled and white, and one on her nose that was a colour Twig had never even seen before. It hurt to look at it, it was so disgusting.

Nasty, in the meantime, had taken out the other hiding hag with some kind of hex that had turned the poor hag's entire body purple and made her swell up like a blueberry. That left only the two of them. Sister faced sister across the hag-strewn field.

"Do you give, sister?" asked Nasty.

"Give?" asked Vile, like it was a word she had never heard before.

"Well, I *am* the elder," said Nasty, "and obviously the *better* hag. Just look at you! You're back to like you were before!" She shook her head, her dirty, greasy hair tumbling about.

"Oh, dear," said Witch Wormwood.

"Don't you listen to her, Vile!" yelled Twig, his fingers twitching.

"Yeh, don't listen to her, ye wee hag! Ye can take her!" shouted Glimfinkle.

Nasty turned to glare at them. "Stay out of it, you lot! You're not a Hornwort."

"No, but *I* am," said Vile, with such force that Nasty spun back round to look at her. But she wasn't fast enough. Vile cast a curse Twig had never seen her use before. He could almost see it as it hurtled towards Nasty like a slightly invisible arrow. Hag magic wasn't the same as wizard magic, but there were definitely common elements. Whatever it was she had thrown, it was big magic.

It hit Nasty square in the face, knocking her off her feet and flat on to her back. She rolled over and crawled on to her knees, her hands scrambling all over her face. "What did you DO?" she wailed. "How COULD you?" She stood up, inadvertently showing everyone what Vile had done.

Gone were all of Nasty's warts. Her crooked nose had been straightened. Her teeth were even and white as pearls. She was as beautiful as any princess locked away in a tower for safekeeping by a misguided king.

"I'm RUINED!" she wailed, throwing her hands over her face. She ran from the field and, just like that, the hag scrap was over and it was clear the best hag had won.

22

IN WHICH SUMAC HAS HIS REVENGE

There was much celebration that night in Witch Wormwood's caravan. There was a feast with everything from bullfrog in the hole (much like toad in the hole but a lot more warty) to sticky pixie dust pudding. Beaky ate more than his fair share and grew large enough that he had to waddle out the door and make himself comfortable on the roof. Witch Wormwood cackled when Twig finally explained the magpie's situation. At least he still looked like a magpie, though his eyes had turned a disconcerting shade of deep red.

A number of still-recovering hags came by to pay

their respects to Vile, though a few left when they caught sight of Beaky on the way in. Vile removed her curses from them, so long as they sufficiently grovelled first. Nasty wasn't among them. Witch Wormwood said she'd heard through the witch grapevine that Nasty had left the Euphonium completely, though no one knew where she'd gone. Vile acted like she didn't care, but Twig noticed she looked up every time the door opened.

A few wizards stopped by as well, including Kudzu of the Spire. He had won all of his matches, with great distinction – and less mess than Twig. The half-elf wizard was very imposing in person: tall, thin and more regal than King Mervyn. He was still trailing flowers and ivy behind him. Mostly bluebells, but also forget-me-nots and an occasional rosebush, which was highly inconvenient but very pretty.

"I must say, very well done, that bit with the spellcatcher," said Kudzu to Twig. "I always knew Pyrite was a dirty cheat." The wizard leaned closer, his beard so pointy that it made Twig wonder whether the wizard's chin was pointed as well. "He's been banned from next year's Euphonium. Not happy about that one bit, I imagine, but it's his own fault. Cheaters never prosper, you know. As should be, as should be."

Twig rather liked Kudzu. The older wizard reminded him of Ripplemintz, except he was much more likely to complete a spell without it blowing up on him. Twig imagined that if Kudzu had made a robe out of phoenix feathers that they would have actually been phoenix feathers. Glimfinkle, however, didn't seem to approve and stood cross-armed and off to the side, glaring at the half-elf until the wizard bowed his thanks to Witch Wormwood for the hospitality and left.

"Good riddance," said the gnome, once the wizard was well out of hearing range.

"I thought he was quite nice," said Twig.

"Elves ain't like people. They might *look* a bit like people, but they ain't. Not like gnomes either. You can't trust 'em."

"Can't trust gnomes?" asked Vile innocently.

Glimfinkle glared at her. *"Elves,"* he said darkly.

"He's only *half* elven," said Twig. "And he's the first

wizard I've met here that seemed decent."

"That's wizards for you," said Witch Wormwood with a tiny grin. "Present company excepted, of course."

Twig woke up the next morning feeling groggy from too much dandelion juice and rainbow candyfloss. He'd had so much sugar and the party had gone on for so long that he'd only slept for a couple of hours. Vile had fallen asleep sitting up, not even making it to bed, and Glimfinkle had curled up in the middle of a loaf of bread left out on the table. Beaky had made himself a nest of sorts on top of Witch Wormwood's caravan. His trilling snores echoed down the chimneys. They let him sleep because no one wanted to wake him.

Given all that, Twig was not looking or feeling his very best for his next duel. He hadn't even had a chance to look up who he'd be duelling, so it was with not a small amount of dismay that he arrived at the pitch to find Sumac Crabapple leering at him from the other side.

"Leaf of Muckwood!" announced Wizard Root.

"Twig," said Twig firmly.

"I told you, my name is *Root*," said the wizard testily. "All you young wizards are the same! No respect!" He stomped off.

Twig sighed.

"Don't worry about it," said Vile through a yawn she didn't bother trying to cover up. "You want me to curse him for you?"

"No," said Twig. After all, he'd been called much worse than "stick" and "leaf" by his brothers. But Vile would have been really handy to know back when he was still living at home.

"He's bound to cheat, that Sumac," said Glimfinkle. "Don't trust him for even a minute."

"Maybe," said Witch Wormwood, "but the judges are really keeping an eye on things after that spectacle with Pyrite." She pointed out various official-looking wizards positioned around the pitch. They hadn't been around during the previous matches. Some Twig recognized as old and venerable wizards from illustrations he'd seen in Ripplemintz's subscription to the *Wizard Quarterly*, still respected though now retired. There were only so many actual jobs for practising wizards, as there were only so many kingdoms. Most kings only kept one on staff, though a few of the very rich kingdoms like Aramore had a full complement of them.

"Anyway," said Vile, "*I'll* be keeping an eye on him too. If he so much as looks at you sideways, he'll regret it!" She cracked her knuckles and a few people nearby backed away. They'd obviously seen the hag scrap.

"We all will," said Witch Wormwood. She patted Twig on the shoulder. "You'll do fine, Twig."

Twig felt a small lump in his throat that had nothing to do with the impending match. He cleared it away and marched out on to the pitch, taking his place on the mound. He wouldn't let them down. And he wouldn't let Sumac win.

Sumac was already in position. He bowed to the judges and then to the crowd, but they didn't cheer for him, except for a couple of stupendously ugly hags. There was a bit of nervous applause but it died down quickly. Twig bowed to the judges as well, but didn't bother bowing to the crowd, so it took him by surprise when a slightly confused cheer of "Twig", "Stick" and "Leaf" went up. He looked to the waiting crowd and saw a group of shouting peasants holding cow hides or sheets or even wearing extra-wide straw hats like they were prepared for anything that might be flung their way. "Dung him!" one man shouted. "Dung him good!" The people around him erupted into louder cheers.

Well, at least he had some people cheering for him, even if they weren't sure of his name. Sumac didn't look pleased by this at all and, as Salamar's hand fell to mark the beginning of the duel after they had bowed to each other, Sumac immediately cast a nasty-smelling foul-wind spell at Twig clearly intended to blow him over.

Twig quickly rooted his feet to the ground with a hastily mumbled, *"Root my boots."*

He was blown about but managed to stay on the mound. But he didn't have time to congratulate himself as Sumac cast another spell immediately. And then another and another and so on. Twig had just enough

time to react but
not enough time
to do any attacking
of his own. That
wasn't what worried
him, though. It was
the spells Sumac was
casting. They weren't the type
of spells he would have expected
from a wizard like Sumac. They were
powerful enough, certainly, but they were very
straightforward. A fireball. A jagged streak of lightning.
A small tornado that tore up the ground around the
pitch. There was nothing sneaky or underhand about
them at all. It was very worrisome. What was he up to?

"Dung him already!" screamed the man in the
crowd. Some other people took up the chant and soon
all anyone could hear was "Dung! Dung! Dung!"

Sumac made a face. Twig wasn't sure if it was a
grin or a grimace. It might have been both. He braced
himself, but instead of casting another fireball or a
blast of frigid air at him, Sumac took a deep breath and

gathered himself much like Ripplemintz did before he was about to cast something biggish. Twig doubled his shield.

Sumac worked his hands like he was winding up a big ball of invisible yarn, beads of sweat gathering on his forehead, and then threw the ball of nothing towards Twig. At first, Twig and the rest of the crowd thought that the spell had failed. Nothing happened. No sparks, no fireworks, no dust cloud. Then Sumac pulled at the nothing and Twig felt something inside him twist and twinge. Something warm and fizzy and very deep inside of him. Something he'd only really noticed once Ripplemintz's accidental spell had become part of him.

Sumac made another face and this time Twig could definitely tell it was a grin, a very nasty grin. Sumac yanked again on the nothing he held and

begin reeling it in like he'd hooked a record-breaking fish. The something inside of Twig twanged and stretched like a guitar string pulled taut. The beads of sweat on Sumac's forehead turned into rivulets. The cries of "Dung!" died out as the crowd watched the silent but sweaty tug of war with more than a little confusion.

"That's Nix's Unravelling! He's illegal spellcasting!" one of the sideline wizard judges – a very old and distinguished looking one – yelled out. "I command you to cease immediately!" There was a buzz from the judges' table and from the crowd. Salamar stood up and pointed a very threatening finger at Sumac, but the wizard didn't stop what he was doing. Twig felt dizzy and confused, but he stood rooted to the spot thanks to his earlier spell. He took his hands and waved them in front of himself where whatever Sumac was doing to him should be, but he didn't feel anything, not even the whisper of an invisible thread. He could feel it to his core, though. Whatever it was, it was hooked deep inside him.

"You WILL stop!" rang out Salamar's voice with

great authority.

Sumac, sweat still pouring out of him, just laughed. "Not a chance," he said through gritted teeth. "This boy's got power and it will be mine!"

Twig heard Vile let out a bloodcurdling hag war cry and attempt to cast something at Sumac. But the protections put on the pitch against outside influences held, and whatever she had cursed Sumac with bounced off without doing him any harm. The same precautions held the officiating wizards at bay, each one watching in horrified fascination at the scene unfolding in front of them.

Sumac was trying to steal Twig's magic, just like he'd once stolen his own gran's.

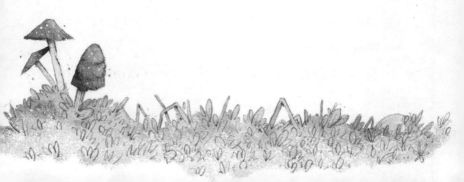

23

IN WHICH TWIG FINDS
WHAT HE NEEDS

Twig felt unstuck, a bit like he was being turned inside out, even though from the outside, everything looked fine. The crowd was confuddled; as far as they could tell, the two duelling wizards were merely standing opposite each other and not really doing much of anything. But they knew something was going on because all of the wizards outside the pitch looked a bit sick, like they were watching a giant pull the legs off a pony.

"Do something, Twig!"

Twig wasn't sure if the yell came from Witch

Wormwood or Vile or even Glimfinkle. He blinked and tried to focus but he suddenly felt so tired and it occurred to one small corner of his brain that what Sumac was doing to him was something he'd been trying to do to himself ever since they had left Muckwood: get rid of his magic. Go back to just being plain old Twig without anyone wanting anything from him and kings not knowing who he was and no one in particular trying to kill him or beat him or eat him or, well, anything really. Like how it had been before Ripplemintz's wishful thinking accidental spell, when no one had cared about him at all.

Everything was awfully blurry and felt really far away, everything except for Sumac, who seemed quite close, even though neither one of them had actually moved. Twig felt he could see his magic now, stretched out between them like a long, thin piece of fraying twine. He tried to focus his eyes on Sumac. The wizard was literally drenched in sweat. The horrendously large boil on the tip of his nose jiggled and flopped about like a dead fish.

Twig idly wondered if the boil was going to pop

again. *That* had been a mess. He and Vile had worked for ages to get that cleaned up. It had been disgusting but, at the same time, it had been rather fun. Vile had cracked some incredibly foul jokes the entire time and Twig had laughed so hard that he'd thought he might pee his pants.

There was another angry shout, this time definitely from Vile, and Twig blinked again, his eyelids heavy. He wasn't sure what she'd even yelled out. Something about being strong or needing a swift kick on his rear – he wasn't sure which and, knowing Vile, it could be either. Or both. What had he done before he'd known Vile? And Glimfinkle? What had he been?

Nothing.

He reached out his hands again, feeling like he was pushing through a vat of congealed stew, and this time he grabbed hold of the fast-unravelling thread of magic stretched between himself and Sumac, who was still reeling it in as fast as he could. He couldn't really see it or feel it properly, but he *knew* it was there and it was his – *not* Sumac's – and he grabbed on and pulled back. Sumac grunted in surprise and his eyes bugged out momentarily, then narrowed as he dug his heels in and pulled harder. But now Twig had a hold on himself and he didn't let go.

The crowd was chanting again, led by Witch Wormwood. "Twig! Twig! Twig!" they shouted. Each time they said his name, he wound up another bit of himself. His feet stayed rooted to the ground, but Sumac was beginning to come unbalanced as Twig pulled and pulled.

Twig concentrated harder, trying to clear his fuzzy mind of everything but what he was doing.

The black-clad wizard fell to his knees.

Twig closed his eyes and pictured his friends. Even in his imagination Vile was yelling at him to *pull harder, you idiot*. So he pulled with everything he had, this time from inside himself.

With a frustrated cry, Sumac tumbled from the mound.

The pitch protections fell and all of Vile's pending curses – she'd been flinging them with wild abandon the whole time – descended upon the wizard at once.

The last bit of Twig's magic twanged and snapped

back with a *crack* and a *pop* that knocked Twig clean out of his boots. The last thing he saw before he closed his eyes was Vile's face swimming towards his own in the midst of all the chaos.

It was Vile's fault that Sumac escaped. The final curse she had flung at him was the infamous Henbit Chicken Curse, which was fitting, as Sumac's own nan had refined it to the art form that it was. Sadly, it was also what enabled him to take flight in all the confusion as everyone rushed the pitch.

Twig, of course, didn't know any of this until much later, when he awoke in unfamiliar but very sumptuous surroundings. He was lying on silk and velvet cushions in a large tent dimly lit by candles. He sat up, rubbing his head. It ached.

"He's awake!" screamed Vile, which made his head hurt even more than it already did.

"You must relax and take it easy, Wizard Twig," said a deep voice with so much authority that Twig nearly lay back down again. It was the wizard Salamar.

Twig looked around cautiously. It wasn't only

Salamar who was there. The other judges were as well: Haggis of Aramore twiddling with the end of his long beard as he peered curiously at Twig from underneath his hairy eyebrows, and the People's Wizard, Moss Milkweed, smiling kindly at him while perched on top of a precarious pile of cushions. He was a tiny, wiry man, dwarfed next to Salamar.

"How are you feeling?" asked Milkweed.

"Like a bloomin' troll sat on my head," said Twig without thinking, then he blushed when he realized who he was speaking to. "I mean, my head hurts a bit, is all."

"As well it should," said Haggis of Aramore, tossing his beard over his shoulder like a scarf. "You realize, I hope, that no one has ever survived a successful casting of Nix's Unravelling before, don't you? It's a wonder you're alive at all, my boy."

"A true testament to your will," said Salamar.

Glimfinkle jumped up on to Twig's knee. "The question is, can ye still do magic?"

"Glimfinkle!" That was Witch Wormwood. She swatted the gnome off of Twig's knee and he bounced off a cushion and rolled on to the floor, but popped back up immediately with a *sproing*.

"Wot? It's what ye all want to know, isn't it?" he grumped. "S'all ye been talkin' about fer the last hour."

"So can you?" asked Vile. She was standing off to the side, looking especially grimy against the backdrop of the fancy judges' tent. At least she wasn't yelling any more.

Twig sat up straight, which was a bit difficult on the slippery silk cushions. He looked inside himself. There was no empty hole, no void. He felt full of light and sound and fury and fizz. *"Let there be light,"* he spelled, and all the candles in the tent flared up as one, making it brighter than the brightest day the kingdoms had ever seen.

Later that night, it was Glimfinkle that reminded Twig that there was still one last duel to go. Kudzu had won his third round duel in an upset against the usually unbeatable Pumice Pummelstone of Aramore. It was to be the half-elf wizard that would meet Twig in the final competition. Twig had been declared the winner against Sumac, even though it hadn't at all been a normal duel.

After all, he'd survived.

"Ye sure yer all right, boy? I got a fair bit of coin on ye, ye know." Glimfinkle shook his tiny bag of holding, and the coins inside jingled. Twig had had to enchant a bag for him in order to hold all his previous winnings.

"I'm fine," said Twig. All of the judges had inspected him more thoroughly than he'd ever imagined possible, Witch Wormwood had dosed him with smelly poultices and gloppy potions he'd rather not remember the taste of, and even Vile had performed a cleansing curse removal on him just in case. Mostly, Twig wanted to go to sleep. It felt like every wizard at the Euphonium had come by to look at him to see who had survived Nix's Unravelling, even Wizard Root. Normally, someone beating Pumice of Aramore would have been the talk of the Euphonium, but none of this was normal.

There was a heavy knock on the door.

"*Ahem.*" It was the most imperious-sounding throat clearing Twig had ever heard. Simon Pennyroyal stood in the door, his nose in the air like he was trying not to breathe in.

"King Mervyn to see Twig of Muckwood," he announced solemnly.

"The *Wizard* Twig," said Vile firmly.

"Er . . . the Wizard Twig," said Pennyroyal, looking disgruntled but attempting a smile.

He stood aside and the king, his eyebrows looking even sharper than Twig remembered, stepped inside. Dressed in his silks and furs, he looked very out of place in the hodgepodge of Witch Wormwood's caravan. Ripplemintz came in behind him, wearing his bedraggled not-quite-phoenix feather robe. He gave Twig a smile and a nod.

Twig nervously scrambled to his feet and was going to attempt a bow until Vile elbowed him with a frown and a look that very clearly said *You're the world's most powerful wizard! Stop bowing and scraping!*

"Well," said King Mervyn, looking around the caravan with barely concealed revulsion, "I understand you have acquitted yourself quite well thus far in the competition, boy."

Vile snorted and would have said something likely to be rude, but Witch Wormwood jumped in a bit more politely. "He survived Nix's Unravelling, your majesty!" Pennyroyal glared at her for speaking out of turn.

Ripplemintz cleared his throat. "That has *never* been done before, your majesty."

The king shot the sage a look that clearly said he didn't like being interrupted. He looked Twig in the eye. It was a very sharp look that made Twig wish he *had* bowed, no matter what Vile thought. "I trust you will continue your success and win this competition for the glory of your kingdom."

"Er . . ." said Twig.

"Your family awaits news of the duels most anxiously," said Pennyroyal smoothly.

"Are they here?" squeaked Twig, surprised. Had they actually come to see him?

"Oh no," said the king. "They remain at the castle, but I am certain they are here with you in spirit."

Did the king mean they were actually *in* the castle? Twig couldn't picture it. *Where* in the castle exactly? Surely not the nice part. He looked at Ripplemintz, who shook his head slightly, and then Pennyroyal, but the unctuous man merely smiled thinly at him. He looked like a codfish.

The king chuckled then, making Twig twitch. "I stopped in to pay my respects to the rulers of Humble, Goldlocke and Bragmore on the way here," he said. His smile was as cutting and sharp as the rest of him. "I should very much like to pay my respects to the Spire as well. Are you ready for your match tomorrow, boy?"

Twig wanted to say no, because, truthfully, he

hadn't had much time to think about it. But he couldn't say that, not with the king looking at him that way. "Yes, your grace," he said instead, trying to sound confident and secure, like he imagined a powerful wizard like Kudzu would sound.

"Good." The king's smile grew. "We must talk, you and I, after the Euphonium." He shot a glance at Pennyroyal. "The kingdom with the most powerful wizard in all of the kingdoms ... well, let us say that there is much we could accomplish, boy."

"*Wizard*," muttered Vile, mostly under her breath, but the king heard her anyway.

"Yes," he said, waving a hand vaguely in the air. "Indeed." He turned towards the door, nearly running into Ripplemintz, who stepped quickly out of the way. The king frowned at the sage. "I must admit, I had never *appreciated* what magic could do before, but I am beginning to see the possibilities." He looked back at Twig. "Thanks to you, young wizard."

"We look forward to your performance tomorrow," said Pennyroyal, as the king swept out of the door. "Much depends upon it." He followed the king out.

"Well done, Twig," said Ripplemintz. "I'm quite proud of you."

"Thanks," said Twig. The words felt like a real compliment coming from the sage.

"Never thought you'd make it this far! Quite an accomplishment!"

"Er ..." said Twig. He wished Ripplemintz had stopped talking a couple of sentences back.

"Ripplemintz!" called Pennyroyal from outside. "The king wants a tour!"

"Must dash," said the sage, backing out of the door and nearly tripping in his hurry. "Trying to keep my job and all that ..."

"Good luck with that," said Glimfinkle.

24

IN WHICH THE END BEGINS

The king had departed quickly, but Twig had trouble getting to sleep after his visit. What the king had said was worrying enough, but it was all the things he *hadn't* said that were keeping Twig awake. What kind of plans did the king have exactly? Was Twig's family OK? What about Ripplemintz? Did the wizard know that Twig didn't want his job? More importantly, did the king know that?

He lay there wondering if he should have let Sumac steal his magic after all. Surely the king wouldn't have been able to blame *that* on him, and his family would have been safe from courtly intrigue, *and* he wouldn't be lying awake wondering what exactly the king wanted him to do with his power. Of course, if he *had* let Sumac steal his magic, he probably wouldn't still be around to wonder all these things, so he really couldn't complain.

Not to mention what a wizard like Sumac might have done with that kind of power. Witch Wormwood was right: most wizards couldn't be trusted any further than you could throw them. Twig hadn't met many that he liked, he realized, and he'd met even fewer that he trusted. There was the People's Wizard, of course, but he was ancient. Twig wasn't sure about Salamar. He'd seemed nice enough, in a slightly scary stern-uncle sort of way. But was he really half efreet? Because you couldn't trust an efreet. They'd burn you up as soon as look at you. That was what people said.

Ripplemintz was decent enough but the thought of him with unlimited power was a bit frightening. The damage he did was contained mostly because he wasn't very good at what he did and he didn't want anything beyond what he already had. Kudzu of the Spire was the only wizard Twig had met that didn't make him feel a bit terrified inside. Maybe it was the flowers. You couldn't *not* like a wizard who spread beauty. Well, Vile could, but normal people couldn't.

Twig finally fell asleep mid-thought and woke up the next morning still thinking it. He held on to that thought through breakfast and through Glimfinkle giving him a pep talk and even through Witch Wormwood's last bit of advice and a dose of tonic that tasted like bad dreams and half-rotten cabbage. Only Vile seemed to notice how preoccupied he was.

"It'll all be fine," she told him as they walked to the pitch for the final duel. "And if it isn't, we'll curse 'em and get out of here."

"Yeah," he said, still thinking his thought.

"Ye got it, boy," said Glimfinkle, sitting on Vile's shoulder and holding on to her hair. "Ye'll wipe the pitch with that half-elf ninny."

"Cheer up, Twig," said Vile. "You're the most powerful

wizard in all the kingdoms. There's nothing you can't do, right? And Kudzu isn't known for being particularly, er, violent. He beat Pumice by overwhelming him with vines. And not even choking stinkweed – vines with *flowers*."

"Yes. Right," he said. The thought he'd been having bloomed a bit more. He wondered what Vile would think of the idea he'd had about the duel. He didn't think she would like it. But then there wasn't time to ask or think of something else. In fact, it was nearly impossible to think at all because of the noise that arose as they arrived.

The pitch was absolutely surrounded by a mob of people at least fifty deep, but they parted easily in front of him, cheering as he came, and this time with his actual name. Even more people were seated in some hastily erected stands. It seemed like all of the kingdoms were there. Certainly all the ones who could be there, were. It might have been the most-attended duel in Euphonium history.

"Twig of Muckwood!" announced Wizard Root loudly as they approached the opening to the pitch. He patted Twig on the back like they were the best of friends. "You should have told me I had your name wrong," he said in a wounded voice. "Good luck today! We're all cheering for you!"

"Yes. Right," said Twig again. He turned to Vile. "Well," he said, "this is it, I guess—" He broke off, surprised as she grabbed him up in a hug that was over so quickly he wasn't entirely sure it had happened.

"Good luck," she said and pushed him towards the pitch.

He stumbled in and walked slowly to the mound. His old boots were still sitting there, stuck to the ground. None of the wizards had been able to unroot them from their spot. Witch Wormwood had given him a brand new pair of troll-hide boots to replace them. They smelled a bit, but they would never wear out. He took position behind his old boots in hopes that he wouldn't trip over them if he could see them.

Kudzu of the Spire entered the pitch, waving amid cheers and flowers thrown by his supporters, which mixed in with the ones still sprouting up in his wake. His flower spell was fading. Gone were the roses and fancy lilies. Now the carpet of greenery he left behind was merely clover and a daisy here and there. He waved cheerfully to Twig. "Good luck to you," he called over.

"And you," yelled back Twig. He looked to the judge's platform. King Mervyn was seated there for the final duel, as was Queen Carnelian of the Spire. Where Kudzu was only half elf, she was fully elven and had an unearthly beauty about her that was obvious even across the field. Her silvery eyes narrowed briefly as she caught Twig's eye, and she inclined her head in acknowledgement. Twig swallowed. He felt like she'd just stolen a glimpse inside his soul. Maybe that was what Glimfinkle had meant. Elves definitely weren't the same as people.

"Are the wizards ready?" Salamar had spelled his voice so that it boomed over all the noise everyone was making. The cacophony died down a bit as all eyes turned towards the pitch.

Twig swallowed and nodded. It was now or never. He'd always thought that was a bit of a silly saying before but now he understood it.

Salamar's hand lowered and the duel was on.

Twig wanted to see what Kudzu's magic *felt* like. You could tell a lot about a wizard by his casting. Sumac's spells were dark with envy and hate at their core. Pumice's had left the sound of applause ringing in his ears and felt full of grand plans and empty promises. Tansy had been direct and no-nonsense, but had the smell of slightly burnt toast. What was Kudzu's like? Especially when he was casting against another person?

For a moment, neither of them did anything. Kudzu almost seemed like he was waiting to give him first go, but after Twig didn't do anything, the half-elf nodded to himself and cast out a blanket of snapdragons that spread through the pitch. The crowd let out a collective gasp as the flowers grew all the way to the fence that held them back. At first, the flowers just looked pretty, but then the ones nearest Twig began snapping at his feet, letting out little growls as they came up against the impenetrable troll hide of his boots.

Twig took a deep breath in. Kudzu's magic smelled of flowers and sunshine and lazy afternoons.

With this clap, you have no snap.

Twig cast, clapping his hands together. The biting

snapdragons turned into normal flowers, their cheerful heads bobbing in the slight breeze. There was a smattering of applause from the spectators.

Twig looked across the pitch at Kudzu. He was clapping along with the crowd and smiling at him. Was the wizard going easy on him?

Twig needed to know. What was Kudzu capable of? Maybe he should fight fire with fire. Or, in this case, flowers. Twig cast the spell nice and loud.

Primose grows whither thou goes!

A blanket of primroses began to grow all around Kudzu, starting at his feet and then taking root and creeping up his cloak and robes. The wizard watched as they grew, a wide smile upon his face.

"Lovely!" he called to Twig, "Just lovely! Very well done!" He let them grow up to his waist before he muttered a spell to stop them spreading.

"It's not a bloomin' flower festival," yelled Glimfinkle from the sidelines. "Get on with it, ye silly wizards!"

Twig had seen enough. He was ready to do what needed to be done, but so was Kudzu.

The half-elf wizard began casting out some rapidly

growing vines towards him but Twig ignored them as they grew and squiggled among the flowers on the pitch between them almost like snakes. He had to concentrate on what *he* was casting. He'd been thinking about it last night, and even while he slept. He'd been thinking about it all morning. He couldn't get this one wrong.

With careful precision, Twig sang out each line of the spell loudly so that everyone could hear. Especially King Mervyn.

> *"A slight exaggeration was the cause of my*
> *frustration,*
> *But too much magic is tragic.*
> *So with this spell, I right a mistake,*
> *And make a gift of what another tried to take.*
> *No longer the most powerful,*
> *May my magic become most . . . flowerful!"*

It was the longest spell Twig had ever cast, but, then, it was also the most important. He didn't really like the end, but it had been all he could think of to rhyme with powerful, and it reminded him of Kudzu anyway. As he finished the words, he felt that sparkly fizzy something deep inside him twist and knot and then finally split in two with a pop. The bit of magic that flowed out of him travelled up the vines cast by Kudzu, and through the large, colourful flowers that had sprouted as it went. Kudzu abruptly stopped his casting as the fizzing ball of power hit him and disappeared inside. He sat down with a small *"Oof!"* of surprise and then rolled down the mound to lay flat on the pitch.

There was a moment of silence and then a tumult comprised of equal amounts cheering and confusion. The spectators in the crowd weren't sure what he had done. The wizards who had heard what he had cast were aghast and mumbling among themselves. King Mervyn was half stood, trying to figure out what had happened.

Salamar's booming voice rang out. "Twig of Muckwood is the victor!"

Twig found himself surrounded as people swarmed the pitch.

25

IN WHICH THERE IS BOTH
FAME AND GOLD

King Mervyn was both pompously mad and grudgingly happy. He told Twig as much, though not directly. He sent Simon Pennyroyal. The king, Pennyroyal reported, was pleased that a wizard of Muckwood had won at the 100th Euphonium, but peeved that in doing so Twig was no longer the most-powerful wizard in the kingdoms.

"Why did you do it, boy?" asked Pennyroyal. He was a man that had spent his whole life attempting to accumulate power. He couldn't see why *anyone* would give it away, especially in front of other people.

"You try being the world's most

powerful-wizard," said Twig. "See how *you* like it." He was tired and didn't feel like arguing anymore. Pennyroyal wasn't the first person to ask him that question. It seemed that nearly every magic user at the Euphonium wanted to know the same thing. It had taken Twig, Vile, Glimfinkle and Witch Wormwood hours to work their way back to the caravan after the award ceremony.

Pennyroyal shrugged and turned to go. "Wait," said Twig, "what about my family? Will the king release them?"

"*Release them?* From where?"

"Er . . ." said Twig, not sure how to answer.

Pennyroyal laughed heartily. "Oh, dear boy, did you think he had them locked in the dungeons or something? They're camped out in Ripplemintz's tower awaiting your triumphant return." He snorted. "We'll see what kind of welcome they give you once they hear what you did. Well, I suppose there's still the prize money." He bowed and left.

It wasn't entirely true that every magic user at the Euphonium had wanted to know what possessed Twig to do what he'd done. Witch Wormwood hadn't asked and neither had Vile. In fact, they hadn't said a word about it. Even now, they were sitting quietly at the table drinking some rootwood bark tea. Glimfinkle was sat on the corner of the table glumly drinking something that definitely didn't smell like tea. *He'd* asked why Twig had done it. Repeatedly. And called him a few choice words as well. Twig had answered the same thing every time; it had seemed what was best.

Twig swirled his teacup around but didn't drink any. He'd made that mistake earlier and found that rootwood bark tea tasted exactly like it sounded. He was starting to think witches and hags didn't have any taste buds.

"Just say it," he said to Vile when he couldn't take her slurping any more.

"Say what?" she asked.

"That I'm stupid to have given my magic away," Twig said. He was starting to think so himself. After all, could *all* those wizards be wrong? Even Kudzu had asked him why he'd done it, after he had recovered from the shock of it, that is. Then he'd grown himself a long, flowing cape of living flowers and walked off grandly through the crowd without even a thank you.

"You're not stupid," came a voice through the window. The door opened and the oracle came in, leaping lightly over the loose floorboard by the door like she knew it was there.

"What do *you* want?" asked Vile.

Witch Wormwood looked the young woman up and down, taking in her flowing hair and serene expression. "You're the oracle," she said.

"I know," said the oracle.

"Of course you do," said Witch Wormwood, her mouth twitching. "And what can we do for you?"

"It's what *I* can do for you," said the oracle. "I understand there was some confusion over my earlier prophecy."

"No," said Vile tightly, "you were very clear. And you were wrong. I won the hagging, no thanks to you! Some oracle you are!"

The oracle sat down at the table uninvited and poured herself a cup of tea.

"What was the prophecy again?" asked Witch Wormwood.

"She said, *One cannot be what one is not. You are what you are what you are*," said Twig.

"Yes, exactly," said the oracle. "Really, I was *quite* clear."

"Hmmm," said Witch Wormwood. "And the questions?"

"The wee hag wanted to know if she was ever going to be a proper hag. And me, I just wanted to know if I'd ever be as grand as I should be. And Twig here wanted to know how to get rid of his curse," said Glimfinkle.

The oracle tut tutted. "Now now, that wasn't Twig's *real* question," she said. "We all know that. After all," she said, turning to Twig, "you weren't cursed."

"So what do you think my real question was?" he asked.

"Whether or not you really are the world's greatest wizard," she said. "Of course."

"Oh, I see," said Witch Wormwood, nodding her head sagely. It reminded Twig of Ripplemintz when he'd puzzled out a problem.

"See wot?" asked Glimfinkle.

"Vile has *always* been a proper hag," said Witch Wormwood. "And Twig definitely is the world's greatest wizard. No one has ever survived Nix's Unravelling before or managed to cast a spell like you did in that last duel." She wagged a finger at Twig. "Magic can't live where it has no home," she said. "Accidental spell or not, Twig, the magic was in you. In fact, I'd go so far as to say that there are no accidents. Not really. You *are* who you are. *All* of you are."

"Exactly," said the oracle. "I knew you'd understand."

"Of course you did," said Witch Wormwood, her grin not even hidden now.

"Oh," said Vile, shifting in her seat like she wasn't sure if she felt like cursing someone or not.

"Well, maybe," said Twig grudgingly. "That's who I *was*. I *was* the greatest wizard, for a while. Now I'm just Twig again."

"Are you saying I'm wrong?" asked the oracle. She put down the cup of tea she'd been about to drink from, which was the smartest thing Twig had seen her do yet.

"But I gave away my magic to Kudzu," said Twig.

"All of it?" asked the oracle, with a faint smile.

Twig thought about what he'd felt when the fizziness inside him had split into two. Only the smaller bit had gone to Kudzu. He could still feel his magic inside him. It felt warm. "No, not all of it," he said finally. "Just a small bit of it."

"Ye didn't?" asked Glimfinkle, sitting up straight.

"And surely you don't think that all it takes to be the world's greatest wizard is power? That's just silly. What's power got to do with who you *are*?"

"Er . . ." said Twig.

The oracle giggled. "You'll see," she said. "I'm always right."

"Of *course* you are," said Witch Wormwood. "You are the oracle." She was enjoying the situation entirely too much.

"And now I must go," said the oracle. "There's somewhere I have to be." She stood up and then paused, tapping a finger against her temple. "I see that we'll be running into each other again." She nodded to herself and smiled. "And so I shall give you a parting prophecy, as it looks like you'll need it." She sent a sweeping look around the table that took in all of them at once and proclaimed: "You must find beauty where there is none."

Then she took herself off so quickly they didn't have time to ask any questions, leaving behind her undrunk tea, one laughing witch and three open mouths.

"Ye know, I been thinking," said Glimfinkle after a moment, still staring at the door.

"Really?" said Vile. She had a big grin. "That sounds dangerous."

The gnome ignored her. "Yeh, I have. If the oracle's right, and yer a proper hag and Twig's still a proper great wizard, most powerful or not, what's to say I can't be grand?"

"Well, you're certainly not humble," said Vile.

"And why should I be? I'm destined for great things, ye know. I can feel it in me bones. That's why I'm stickin' with the two of ye."

"*What?*" said Twig and Vile at the same time.

"Thinks about it. Yer bound to be havin' more adventures, right? And that's where the fame is, me lad, that's where it's at."

He jiggled his bag of holding. Even be-spelled as it was, it was heavy with coin. "And not just fame, o' course. There's gold to be had!" he said, with great satisfaction.

In which thanks and acknowledgements are made to:

My amazing writing group for keeping me (mostly) sane:
Tracey Mathias, Candy Gourlay, Sara Grant,
and Gail Doggett.

My editor, Fiz Osborne, for always being a supporter and
a believer (and for her cool hair, which I am so jealous of).

My agent, Ben Illis, for being Twig's (very tall) champion.

My fellow writers Brian Farrey and Catherine Ryan Hyde
and our yearly bet, which I nearly always lose and most
especially to Catherine, since she's the one who gave me
the title that eventually led to this story.

My old friend Jaymi Curley for knowing the ascending order of familial gnome naming conventions, even though
I've never known her to wear a pointed red hat.

Karen Kincy for figuring out that a hag named
Vile (Viola) would, by necessity, need a sister
called Nasty (Nasturtium).

Timothy Brannan for knowing so much about spells
and witches and how best to unravel them.

100th Annual Euphonium Wizard Duel Bracket

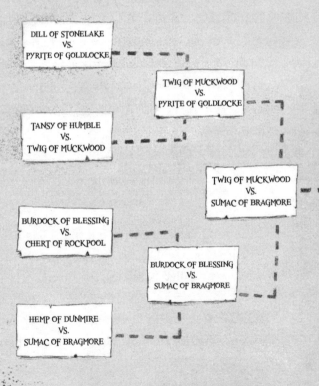

DILL OF STONELAKE
VS.
PYRITE OF GOLDLOCKE

TWIG OF MUCKWOOD
VS.
PYRITE OF GOLDLOCKE

TANSY OF HUMBLE
VS.
TWIG OF MUCKWOOD

TWIG OF MUCKWOOD
VS.
SUMAC OF BRAGMORE

BURDOCK OF BLESSING
VS.
CHERT OF ROCKPOOL

BURDOCK OF BLESSING
VS.
SUMAC OF BRAGMORE

HEMP OF DUNMIRE
VS.
SUMAC OF BRAGMORE

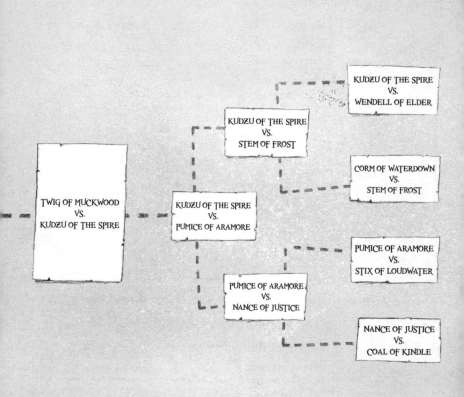

KIMBERLY PAULEY wanted to grow up to be Douglas Adams, Robert Heinlein, or Edgar Allen Poe when she was little, but has since settled for being herself and writing her own brand of quirky. Born in California, she has lived across the United States, but now makes her home in the United Kingdom, along with her husband (a numbers man) and son (her partner in crime).

She is the award-winning author of four YA novels. Her first novel, *Sucks to Be Me* (called a "vampire bat mitzvah novel" by her husband), was an ALA Quick Pick for Reluctant readers, while the sequel, *Still Sucks to Be Me*, was a VOYA Sci-Fi/Fantasy Best Title.

Ask Me received a star review from Booklist and is set in her native Florida (the backwoods bit, not the beaches). *The Accidental Wizard* is her first middle grade novel and, perhaps, the most fun to write.

You can find out more at www.kimberlypauley.com or follow her on Twitter (@KimberlyRPauley) or Instagram, where she posts entirely too many pictures of random things (mostly London and the things she makes).